THE RELUCTANT MESSIAH

by **Gregory Seth Harris**

Published by Buster Bodhi Press, LLC

ISBN 979-8-9991504-1-7
Library of Congress Control Number: 2026900714

Edited by Joseph A. Cavanaugh
Cover and book design by Mark Andrew James Terry

Available on Amazon.com, Barnes & Noble online,
and most online book sellers.

TABLE OF CONTENTS

dedicated to
Dante
one of the most
brilliant minds
to have graced this planet

also to
Melinda Mlinac
and
Tupper Cullum
two of the most
radiant souls
to have graced my planet

FOREWORD

I have at times asserted that the key to living in relative peace and harmony with ourselves, our neighbors, our community and the natural course of human existence, has already been stated. Revealed more than a thousand times, in hundreds of languages, in thousands of settings across the globe. Sadly, we usually gravitate to these great truths only during times of great upheaval, or after some devastating catastrophe leaves those affected shell-shocked into finally opening their eyes.

Thus the perpetual need for a Moses, a Jesus, a Mohammad, a Buddha, a St. Francis, a Gandhi, a Martin Luther, a Martin Luther King...the list near endless. Some enlightened spirit to begin again the arduous task of getting humanity back on track—always with great resistance. Even when resurrected, the message is never fully or universally implemented and more than likely, over a few generations, will fall again on many a deaf ear.

Which begs the question: Why bother? Why, when it is a given that such saviors will inevitably be crucified—if not literally, figuratively.

Enter my reluctant messiah.

Seth

There is nothing new
under the sun

I

There is nothing new under the sun
Those who fail to learn from history
Stumble along a forked tongue in the road
The art of the steal
The root of all   evil
Lucifer slips another log on the fire
Ear cocked to the bully   on the pulpit
The little man   thick black mustache
Fist pummeling his palm, face orange with fury
*   as he blames Armageddon*
on liberals, communists, homosexuals
Welcome back. It's Germany, circa 1933
Here's a banana for your republic.
There is nothing new under the sun

The instant I see him I had to follow. I had to.

I yell for the bus driver to stop. I yank the cord but have to wait. A block and a half pass before the bus pulls to the curb. I bound out the backdoor, glancing down the sidewalk. Not taking time to button my coat, I run, holding onto my hat. The crisp air stings my cheeks. In my mind's eye, I see him still: the teal shirt, the dark pants, his curly head of dark hair. There is something about him I can't quite nail down. Something that perked my interest the moment my eye caught his. But I no longer see him. I fear he has gotten away—until. . .

He has crossed the street and is mounting a pyramid of stone steps. Too impatient to wait for the traffic light, I dash across Lincoln Avenue, signaling a car headed toward me to hold up; let me pass. By the time I reach the curb, he has entered the building.

I can't decide if the building is a city building, an old church, or a building that was once a church repurposed to serve some official capacity. It looks, or at least feels, to be somewhat stately. I dash up the steps fearing if I don't hurry, he will duck inside some room and be lost to me forever. Unless I wait at the entrance for him to exit—something I feel half-compelled to do. Despite having no explanation as to why. Why so important to find this man? And what might I say, if anything, when I encounter him?

I stand in the lobby, the floor and walls carved in marble. Or so I imagine. I really know nothing about stonework. I only have the sense the building is old, regal, the architecture tasteful and well-designed. I realize it is some kind of museum. The stone columns have a sheen to them, the ceilings high and arched. An armed guard stands near what looks to be an information desk. The woman seated at the booth is dark-haired and attractive. I feel compelled to approach her but notice most of those in the building, most entering after me, all head in the same direction.

I follow, looking from face to face, hoping for some kind of clue as to what they may share in common. Where they might be heading en masse. Following them down a corridor, I come to the wide-open double doors of a small auditorium. More than half the seats are taken.

I stand in back; unsure I am in the right place. I debate whether a better strategy might be to return to the lobby. What if he leaves the building while I am here witnessing some program, I know nothing about? Yet part of me insists I stay, that I remain inconspicuous and let unfold whatever is about to take place.

More people filter in. I listen to the buzz of various conversations, closing my eyes, picking up words and phrases here and there. Again, I visualize the man I had seen, this time seeing the briefcase or satchel strapped across one shoulder, dangling at his side. I recall the heat that had surged through my scalp a scant instant before my gaze found him, him strutting by, dodging a couple who weren't looking where they were walking, he tipping an invisible hat as they freeze to avert colliding into him.

Recalling the instance, heat again flushes my cheeks. I grow acutely aware of the back wall I press against and a vague sense of electricity crackling in the air. Ushers bring out folding chairs for those of us standing in the back. I thank the chubby-cheeked usher offering me a chair. I sit, head raised high so as to see over those in the last row.

At some point, the lights dim slightly. Someone walks on stage to tap the microphone then retreats to where he had entered. The crowd hushes, though isolated conversations continue as most heads turn toward the stage.

Only tepid applause rings out when the man I had seen on the street approaches the podium. Whether I hear it or imagine it, a portion of the crowd emits barely audible hisses. I get a sense of disdain by some of those around me. I imagine some prepared to hurl objects at him at the slightest provocation. I fix my eyes on him, suddenly apprehensive as to what is about to transpire. No one introduces him.

Good afternoon, he begins. Thank you for being here.

He places both hands on either side of the podium, leaning in as he glances around the auditorium.

The question I have come to address —, he pauses, looking around again. The question I have come to address is: What is God?

It is a question that has plagued humankind, specifically Western man, for millennia—along with its sister question: Does God even exist? Though before answering the latter, we must address the former.

He pauses again, looking around the room which has mostly gone silent.

My take on God, which some of you have previously heard me state, is intricately woven in with my understanding of how language works. I have stated in a previous talk how I consider myself an expert on how language works. Indeed, it is the limitations of language that makes the question *What is God?* such a landmine.

Let me state first: It is important to recognize that words are symbols, which is to say metaphors. What do I mean by this?

Pulling the microphone from its stand, he places it to his chin. He begins to pace the front perimeter of the stage. His free hand gestures as he asserts that the word 'rock' is not a rock.

You can't throw the word rock and hope to hit anything, he says. The word rock is a symbol, a metaphor if you will, to designate that object we can throw or skip over water.

Communication can be pretty straightforward when these symbols called 'words' are used to designate concrete objects. Objects we can see and feel: a rock, a tree, a building. But things start to get sticky when the words, the symbols, the metaphors, are used to designate ideas or concepts; things invisible to the naked eye.

Words like freedom, justice, racism; even simple words like love, guilt, faith. Have you ever tried to engage in an intelligent debate over capitalism vs. socialism? Most such conversations are doomed to failure. No solid understanding or consensus can be reached. That's because words like 'capitalism' and 'socialism' mean vastly different things to the different people using those same two words. Our individual understandings of capitalism and socialism are oftentimes strikingly different. Thus, we often end up talking apples and oranges.

Not only do different people have varying understandings of what these two words mean, but we attach various connotations and associations to those words depending on our upbringing and personal experiences. As Americans, we have been socialized to despise communism and socialism. Those in socialist and communist countries are socialized to despise what their countries call Imperial Capitalism.

I was taught anything associated with socialism or communism was evil. However, in my case, the same people who taught me to despise communism, assured me I was inferior to white people because of my skin color. Once I figured out *this* was a ruse—something the dominant race told themselves, to give themselves permission to treat me as if I *were* inferior—they lost all credibility in my eyes. Thus, I do not treat socialism or socialist ideas with the same contempt many in this culture—many of you I imagine—are inclined to do.

My point here, is we oftentimes use the same words to mean vastly different things, yet assume we are talking about the same thing. This is why—at least one reason—discussions centered around politics or religion typically break down, sometimes in heated disagreement.

And there is no word in the English language that means more different things to more different people than the word 'God.'

People begin to rustle in their seats. A few coughing or leaning over to address their neighbor. He pauses at the edge of the stage, me recognizing that though he is light skinned, the shape of his nose, the thickness of his lips and his thick dark hair did suggest he might be African-American. I was later to learn his father was Black while his mother was Irish.

He proceeds to assert that if one were to gather ten people at random, place them in a room to discuss in detail their concepts of God, you would not get two identical understandings. The same would be true, he argues, were you to gather fifty people or one hundred. He suggests our individual concepts of God might be as individual, as subjective, as our fingerprints.

Nevertheless, he continues, it is possible to sort our varying understanding of God into general broad groupings.

I have, for instance, observed people raised in a Catholic community—whether they be believers, agnostics, or atheists—often share similar overall concepts in their idea of God. No doubt this is true among those who grow up Southern Baptist or as Evangelicals. But even then, two people attending the same church or synagogue, listening to the same sermons week after week by the same priests or rabbis, will gravitate toward striking disparities in their overall conception of God or God's Will, this depending on their distinct personalities as well as their individual intellectual, emotional, psychological, and spiritual development.

Religious conversations are notoriously prone to go awry, particularly among persons of competing or varying faiths—and when contending with those of no faith. A major reason for this is we use the same word, the same symbol, 'God,' but mean different things, these differences sometimes subtle, sometimes strikingly at odds with how others use the same symbol, the same metaphor.

To get closer to what *I* mean by God, I must first distinguish between two overarching competing concepts of what is called God—at least God as conceived in Christianity. One is a God we can only access through Jesus or by becoming a Christian; one we can know only by embracing Jesus as our personal savior. This is a God who writes off the overwhelming majority of humankind in favor of one people. Of the billions of people who have populated this planet, past and present, only a select group can have access to this God and benefit from his Grace.

Contrast this with the concept of God best exemplified—at least to me—by what Jesus called 'God the Father.' The God the Father Jesus spoke of, did not care who you were or where you came from. You could be a tax collector. You could be a Gentile, a prostitute. You could even be a Samaritan. It didn't matter. What mattered to this God was two things. First and foremost, how you treat your fellow human being. And secondly, how you conduct yourself in the world. If you treat other people in the way you yourself wish to be treated, and if you avoid destructive behavior patterns—which is what the sins are all about—you were okay in this God's book no matter who you were.

That is a very different understanding of God's nature than one in which God can only be accessed through Jesus—or Moses or Mohammed. Of the two concepts, the one closest to what *I* attach the word God to, is God the Father.

In reading the Old Testament, I noticed I could clump the varying understandings of God into one of three categories.

The first is a God who embraces all of mankind. The Hebrews who recognized this God, understood God to be in everyone's lives; that God has an infinite number of ways to reveal His will to each and every breathing human being. That should you, as a Hebrew, encounter say someone from China, or India, or an Aztec or Mayan, you would not question that God was as much in their lives as in your own.

The second understanding, is a God who only cares about the Jewish people. The rest of humanity could all rot in Hell as far as this God is concerned. Canaanites, Assyrians, Babylonians are merely pawns in an elaborate, centuries-long game wherein God rewards the Hebrews when they are faithful and severely punishes them every time they stray.

The third understanding, is a God who for some reason chose to reveal Himself first to the Hebrews, then assigned the Hebrews the task of spreading that recognition of God to the rest of the world. Ultimately, once everyone came to recognize and embrace that God, there would be peace on Earth, all of humanity living in harmony and able to re-enter the Garden of Eden—i.e. paradise on earth.

Now you can take this third understanding of God and reconcile it with the first. God is the God of all humanity, and He revealed Himself first to the Hebrews that the Hebrew might spread His word until all of humanity is united in the faith of that one God.

You can reconcile this third understanding to the second: that Hebrews are God's favorite people, and by the Hebrews spreading their awareness of God, all humanity would eventually be embraced by God's favor.

But you would be hard-pressed to reconcile the first understanding with the second: that God is the God of all humanity, yet God's sole interest in humanity is the Hebrew people.

Of these three versions, what *I* call God comes closest to the first: a God of all humanity, capable of expressing His will, His grace, His presence to every member of the human race—the God the Father Jesus spoke of.

I need to state here—he pauses, standing in the middle of the stage—what *I* call God is not something I *believe* in. Rather it is something I *recognize*. What I call God is ultimately ineffable, which is to say, one can't say precisely what it is. Words don't go there. The best anyone has been able to do, is describe what God is *LIKE*; that is, to assign it an image, that image serving as a symbol or metaphor for something that ultimately defies language. This is what all religions do. It is what many, many philosophers and thinkers have done, as well as many so-called less-educated people who on one level or another recognize something that is universal and omnipresent, yet hard to pin down in concrete, everyday language.

In the monotheistic religions, the dominant image used is that of an all-knowing, human-like conscious being, gazing down on us from a place beyond our physical vision. A loving father; for some a Moses-like figure, who metes out rewards and punishment according to how we behave. He knows everything, including what we are thinking, so we can't hide anything from Him. Sooner or later, we must stand in His judgment, reconcile ourselves to His will.

For the Chinese and Asian cultures, the dominant image—at least to my observation—is that of flow. Everything has its flow. As we grow, we flow from an infant into an adolescent, then a teenager, eventually into the adult we become, shaped by our environment and all events affecting us. There is a flow in our relationship to our parents—usually loving at first, and then at times, contentious, possibly hostile; going through all sorts of permutations as we flow into maturity. There is a flow in our relationships with each of our siblings, our teachers, and friends; to our finding an eventual mate. There is a flow in how we navigate each growing pang and to how we gravitate toward our eventual career and chosen purpose. There is a flow to natural events, the rise and fall of civilizations, of social upheaval and eventual reconciliation. There is a flow in everything.

Lao Tzu calls this flow the Tao. Yet he states: the Tao that can be expressed in words is not the eternal Tao. The Tao is only an image, only a way of describing or conceptualizing something that ultimately defies language.

The Hindus, at least to my understanding, use the image of an eternal drama or dance. We each live multiple lives in a perpetual living drama. Like an actor, during each lifetime we take on a new role in an endless play of struggles and triumphs (personal and collective) whose ultimate purpose *is* creation. Each of us is a tiny manifestation of God—no less and no more God than was Jesus—creating our world even as we are a part of it. What we create, our huts and houses, our culture, our architecture, our music, our art, our wars, are all part of God's work, achieved through the drama or dance of living our rocky, often contentious lives.

The Ancient Greeks used a vastly different image to get at what the monotheistic religions came to call Yahweh or God or Allah. Their dominant image was a council of gods and goddesses, with multiple demigods, each representing some aspect of our reality.

Though the majority of Greeks might have believed in the literal existence of the gods, those who understood, knew the ancient gods and goddesses were metaphors, symbols; each intended to represent multiple things. They represent forces in Nature. They represent universal concepts. They represent forces within the human psyche: different personalities, different psychologies as well as different elements of communal society—what we today loosely call interest groups. The gods and goddesses are metaphors ancient observers and thinkers used to get at the very same awareness all great civilizations, as well as all astute humans, have been aware of—yet at pains to express in clear, concrete language.

A commotion had begun. Absorbed as I was in all he was saying, I had been slow to acknowledge the mild rumbling around the room. Several in the audience were staring into buzzing cell phones. Increasingly there was stirring and whispering. Heads turn, many looking toward the back of the auditorium. As the speaker elaborated on Ancient Greece, private conversations erupt around the auditorium. A stagehand dashes onto the stage, whispering to the speaker. Both vacate the stage.

One of the double doors abruptly opens, a guard entering, firmly slamming the door behind him. Motioning someone in back to relinquish her chair, he uses the chair leg to secure the double door. He does the same on the other side. Another official appears from back stage to rush to a side door which he apparently locks. As he does so, the stagehand who had whisked the speaker away returns. Using the microphone, he informs us the building is on lockdown. He urges us to stay calm, to remain as silent as possible. Then we hear shots, the lights in the auditorium going suddenly dead.

You reap
what you sow

ll

There is nothing new under the sun
Those who fail to learn   condemned
King Don   the art of the con
Putting his cloak of unaccountability on
You reap what you sow
What could possibly go wrong?
Philistines storm the castle
Picnic on the White House lawn
Yet you find it a hassle to blame the man behind the curtain
Certain if you give him a get-out-of-jail free card
Well, what could possibly go wrong?
You reap what you sow
There is nothing new under the sun

His name is Marvin Tyrone Walker though I am not to find this out for another week. He is a performer, writer and poet who also lectures and conducts discussions on philosophical and religious topics. A kind of guru in plain clothes. Whenever he speaks others tend to fall silent and listen. I encounter him again, of all places, during a hike.

An old college buddy is visiting from the east coast, his wife and young family in tow. Having grown up near the Grand Tetons, Ron is aching to spend quality time in the Colorado mountains. His wife, burdened with a breast-feeding infant, is not the least bit interested in hiking or camping. She visits her family, while Ron and I indulge in a 3-day excursion through Rocky Mountain National Forest. On our first day, around mid-afternoon, we stumble upon a campground, one not officially designated as such. The moment we spot a motley assemblage of boys and men seated in a circle, I feel a twinge in my stomach. Ron veers to avoid them but I am drawn in their direction. Even through the dense foliage of pine and aspen, I recognize the curly halo of dark hair.

Couldn't be, I tell myself. Yet there he is. Speaking while others attentively listen. I momentarily lose my sense of vertigo, my brain spinning as I use the sticky trunk of a pine tree to steady myself. I wave Ron over, then head for their camp.

Several of those seated glance our way. His back to us, Marvin continues talking.

We reason according to what we desire, he is saying. More precisely, we reason according to what we come to value—which is tied to what we desire. Each of us has his or her personal set of priorities. And we reason according to those priorities.

Jamal, I've heard you at times whine about Sheila, what you call her petty bickering. That's because your wife's values, and thus her desires, lie slightly elsewhere from where some of your values lie. I suspect hers lie more in material comfort, in her family and interpersonal relationships. You on the other-hand value your solitude. You live in your head. You also possess a strong urge to understand and right some of the wrongs you see perpetrated in the world. Thus, you reason differently.

Like you, I have grown up a so-called 'second-class citizen.' Like you, I have experienced firsthand being treated as lesser. And like you, I have felt to my very core such a system is grossly unjust. Thus, I desire a world where such injustice doesn't exist, or is at least minimized. As a consequence, I reason in such a way that would lessen the kind of hurt and injustice I experienced as a child.

But say I grew up *white*. Not only do I never experience firsthand what every Black child in this country experiences, but I take for granted the quote/unquote 'fact' that this is the land of the brave and the home of the free. Thus, any understanding of what my Black friends experience is in the abstract. Yes, I know slavery was wrong. Yes, I recognize that racism is unjust—but having never experienced it firsthand, it is not high on my priority list of things that need correcting. I'm more likely concerned with people like myself being able to carve out a decent living. My priorities, my desires, are centered more around me, my family and people like me.

Now, you take someone who grows up wealthy. Life's a breeze, relatively speaking. You are free to do all kinds of things. Travel the world. Eat at fancy restaurants. Stay at the most exclusive hotels. Purchase anything you want on the slightest whim, things your average worker and even some relatively well-off can only dream about. Those privileges, that lifestyle, is second-nature to you. You take such advantages for granted. Maybe even see it as your birthright. Thus, you will be reluctant to surrender such privileges without resistance or resentment. The experiences of the poor and people like myself, Black or brown people, barely appear on your radar, if at all. As such, your desires cause you to reason in a strikingly different way. There will be little to no concern to address the suffering or injustice experienced by people like me.

Glimpsing Ron and me from the corner of his eye, he smiles and bid us welcome.

I've seen you before, I say. At the museum.

You mean The Museum and Cultural Center?

Yes.

At the time, due to the mayhem, I had failed to learn his name. When I'd returned, the center was taped off. When I called, all I got was an answering machine. The gunman, having killed four people and wounded three, took his own life, his motive never established.

Hesitating a moment, he waves us over. If you'd like to join us, he offers, have a seat. Jamal, if you scoot over one of them can share that log.

As I sit, introductions are made. Ron opts to stand.

Including himself there are seven. Jamal, a short,

husky Black man with a full, dark beard; Andrew, a midget with an uncombed reddish-brown tuft of wild hair, freckles saturating his tawny face; Rikki, whom I first took as a boy, wearing a worn t-shirt that revealed two small bumps I realize are breasts; Rico, brown-skinned with dark penetrating eyes and a thin, neatly trimmed moustache; Harvey, his hair a brilliant white, his cheeks wrinkled and sagging, his eyes a pale, sparkling blue; and Pete, arms covered in tattoos, his facial expression morose if not downright angry, striking me as the misfit in the group.

Marvin calls them a troupe of vagabond performers, provocateurs by some people's account. We do theatrical presentations, he explains. Usually for religious or social justice groups: poetry, parables, stories mixed with music, complete with costumes and props.

Each performance, Harvey adds, is custom-tailored and somewhat ad-libbed. You've wandered into one of our 'consciousness-raising sessions' (He makes air quotes).

Marvin: The question we are exploring, is why so much violence and killing and vitriol in our polarized society? That shooter at the museum, for instance. Why take out people you don't know, then take your own life? Why so much hate and fear?

What I was proposing is Western thinking—what I think of as Western thinking—is hopelessly locked in the either/or paradigm. In the West, we have a tendency to think in terms of either/or. That the solution to any given problem must be either *THIS* or *THAT.*

We tend to view the world as this great machine, Jamal adds. Thanks largely to the influence of science and deductive reasoning. As everything is cause and effect, we figure once we break things down to their basic components, we will then understand how everything works.

Harvey: Problem is, we apply this thinking to the

nonphysical world as well. Our access to God, by that logic, must lie in either *this* religion or *that* religion, this denomination or that denomination. The best economic system must be either capitalism *or* socialism. The best political philosophy must be *either* conservatism *or* liberalism.

Marvin: The current animosity in today's politics, lies in the unquestioned assumption that one side is right, and thus the other side, by definition, must be wrong. While scientific and either/or thinking may apply to the understanding and manipulating of the physical world, it doesn't necessarily hold true to the nonphysical world, the world of abstract principles. Though it has its validity, the scientific way of thinking or of looking at things, is not the only way. Looking at things from solely one angle is limiting. Looking at it from another angle can provide additional insights. It's not that this mechanical approach is the wrong way, or the right way. It's just that it's not the *only* way.

It is not either science *or* religion. These are merely different ways of observing and analyzing the same reality. One takes a materialistic approach, the other a spiritual, moral, or metaphysical approach. And those are not the only two ways.

Harvey: Just as we in the West are locked in the false paradigm of science vs. religion, we are hopelessly locked in the false paradigm of either conservative or liberal, Right or Left.

Marvin: To my mind, at the heart of the liberal perspective, are the twin values of Justice and Equity. The Left recognizes the importance of Justice above all else. Whenever and wherever people are treated unjustly, resentment brews, social tension becoming inevitable. People treated unjustly exhibit less respect for the laws and system they feel treat them unfairly. The longer they are treated thus, the more surely they will lash out. Eventually, they will openly rebel. Sometimes in peaceful protest. Sometimes in armed resistance. Typically, those in power respond by coming down hard to teach protesters a lesson—cracking heads, even firing on peaceful demonstrators.

Harvey: But violence only begets more violence.

Marvin: Exactly. Eventually the social tension will get out of hand, perhaps even result in civil war—a pattern that has repeated itself ad nauseam throughout human history, throughout the entire history of human oppression.

The way to circumvent this pattern is to treat everyone justly, to guarantee equal protection under the law. More importantly, to *enforce* equal protection under the law, not just give it lip service. The liberal perspective recognizes that *above all else,* Justice is paramount in creating and maintaining a healthy, peaceful society.

In addition, the Left recognizes the importance of Equity. By Equity, I mean a social and economic system in which the greatest number of citizens are able to carve out a tolerable standard of living; that the least number of people are trapped in a near-daily struggle to make ends meet. When people—especially large numbers of people—are caught in a life-and-death struggle to merely survive, all types of social repercussions ensue. Such people are more likely to commit crimes and other acts of desperation. Children growing up in poverty will be stymied in their development, not just physically, but emotionally and psychologically. Poverty brings with it all sorts of social ills. Reducing poverty is the surest way to tamp down the cancerous effects people living in poverty inevitably have on any society.

Rico: But it's not possible to eliminate poverty. Even Jesus acknowledged there will always be poor.

Marvin: True. Either by their own poor choices, or

by being caught up in circumstances beyond their control, there will always be those living in poverty.

Rikki: And isn't poverty relative? A poor person in this country can be living almost in the lap of luxury compared to those struggling in other countries.

Marvin: That's true too. Yet, the more conscientiously a society works to reduce its number of poor, the more it can minimize poverty's ill effects. Conversely, the less a society commits itself to reducing poverty, the more surely those ill effects will fester and grow, eating away at that society from within. As I was saying, Equity coupled with Justice are, to so-called liberals, the cornerstones of a thriving, stable society.

Rikki: And the conservative perspective?

Marvin: It seems to me the conservative perspective is centered around the paramount importance of being able to generate wealth. Wealth to a nation is what oil is to a car, what water is to the body, to life itself. A well-oiled car runs smoothly. When the oil runs low, the car performs poorly, eventually grinding to a halt. Without wealth, a person, a community, a society, can only manage to scrape by. It will be subject to the whims of circumstance. Survival becomes touch and go. A couple of poor rainy seasons, a devastating flood or hurricane, an attack from one's enemies, and that's it. Back to square one. Wealth provides a buffer against such misfortune. Wealth enables a society to function smoothly, to run efficiently.

Equally true, a generous application of wealth allows a town, a society, a nation, to achieve great things. All great empires, all great civilizations, became so initially through their ability to generate wealth. Great wealth begets great societies, a decent standard of living, great architecture; it finances scientific and technological breakthroughs, commissions great artists and composers, supports great universities and great thinkers in all fields of knowledge. Great wealth allows a nation to accomplish feats previously viewed as impractical, if not impossible: creating machines that fly, railroads to connect distant cities, canals to shorten trade routes, rockets to land on the moon and Mars; satellites, and giant telescopes capable of probing the outer reaches of our universe. The list is endless. For any nation to achieve its fullest potential, to exceed its potential, it must first be able to generate great wealth.

Likewise, where there is great wealth, there must also be great military might. Without military might, more aggressive nations will muscle in on one's economic interests. Equally likely, a greater military power will invade, take your wealth, and co-opt your culture. History has proven repeatedly, the only way a wealthy nation can guarantee its security against external threats, is to be so militarily powerful, no nation or alliance of nations would dare attack it. Wealth and military might is what I see as the cornerstones of the conservative perspective.

The problem with the conservative perspective—from my perspective, at least—is its unquestioned genuflecting to an either/or mindset. Believing itself unquestionably right in embracing the importance of generating wealth and protecting that wealth through a military second to none, it assumes any competing perspective must be wrong. Justice and social equity have no relevance in their either/or mind set. The Right is blind in its failure to recognize Justice and Equity are *just as important* to a healthy society as generating and protecting wealth.

The Ancient Greeks would be petitioning for balance and harmony. All things in moderation. Conservatism in moderation. Capitalism in moderation. Socialism in moderation. A golden mean. Neither side annihilating or dominating its opponents. Either/or thinking fails to recognize most things exist on a spectrum: not light or dark, but varying shades of light into dark, and dark back into light. Heads may be the opposite of tails, but they are part of the same coin—neither could exist without the other.

Harvey: As light could not exist without dark.

Marvin: Exactly. I contend the fallacy of either/or thinking has been at the heart of countless struggles throughout human history. The us-against-them mentality. During the Reformation it was Protestant vs. Catholic. During the Industrial Revolution, capitalism vs. communism.

Jamal: Now its conservative vs. liberal; Republican vs. Democrat; red vs. blue.

Marvin: Either/or thinking fails to take into account differing sets of priorities. A person focused more on treating all concerned parties with Justice and Equity will have a different set of priorities, thus reason differently from someone concerned merely with his/her own personal or financial advancement. It is not that one perspective is right or necessarily superior, and the other wrong. Rather each perspective aims at a different goal and therefore will advocate for a different solution to achieve whatever that desired goal is.

I raise my hand timidly.

If I may, you say the Right is centered around the importance of generating wealth. I'm sorry but I don't see conservatives thinking that way at all. I see most as just greedy son-of-bitches. They don't care about the poor or about social justice. All they care about is their own selfish greed.

Pete: I agree

Marvin: Again, there's a spectrum. Some conservatives do have a healthy regard for those less fortunate. They balance their own self-interest with matters of Justice and Equity. Others not so much—and in varying degrees. And granted, there are those, many perhaps, who don't give a fig about anyone other than themselves.

I think there is no argument capitalism is the best system devised by humans to generate wealth. I think economic history has proven that. But capitalism, at its extreme, is predatory and detrimental to any social system. Capitalism at its extreme embraces slavery. There is a reason this country had to endure a civil war to extricate itself from the institution of slavery. Slavery was too profitable, too wealth-generating for its proponents to quibble over the moral implications of treating humans like chattel, to concern themselves with the brutally inhuman, dare I say unchristian, treatment of Blacks in perpetuating that system.

When the conscience of this nation could no longer tolerate slavery, capitalist diehards then turned to economic slavery: paying workers a bare minimum, the result being a working population so desperately poor, should any worker deign to complain, he could easily be replaced with someone (usually an immigrant) willing to work for even less—all at the expense of treating the working millions with Justice and Equity.

Rico: Thus, the strikes and riots, the brutal massacres of protesting workers throughout the late 19th and early 20th centuries.

Marvin: Granted. While some embrace the principles of capitalism for its essential role in generating wealth, humans being humans, others embrace it to justify and legitimize their rapacious greed. Their touting conservative ideology is motivated less by the good wealth can do in oiling the wheels of society, and more for the power, privilege and prestige great wealth begets those who possess it.

Me: In other words, they worship the almighty dollar.

Harvey: Love of money being the root of all evil.

Marvin: But keep in mind: any attempt to crush or annihilate the opposing side will only result in the defeated side going underground to lick its wounds before rising again like a phoenix to exact its revenge as mercilessly as it feels it has been treated—and the cycle repeats itself so long as we delude ourselves into believing the best solution to any societal problem is either *THIS* or *THAT*.

As we talk, it begins to sprinkle. At first lightly, even stopping a bit. But grayer clouds continue to roll in, and with them heavier and more insistent drops. Soon we scatter. Ron and I are invited to huddle inside the larger tent with Jamal and Rico. Jamal invites us to stay for supper, suggesting we could camp there for the evening. Ron and I agree.

Once the rain subsides, Rico shows us where we can pitch our tent.

Not the first
time

III

Not the first time
Machiavelli pulled an ace from the middle of the deck
to claim the crown, an orange-faced clown
mumbling Orwellian doublespeak
brewing a stew bubbling with hate
Confusion and chaos   pounding on the gate
Citizens scratch their heads, shrug their shoulders
then ask What's for dinner?
Man does not live by bread alone

Not the first time
An emperor with no clothes
ordered the rounding up of scapegoats
while his minions hump the golden goose
in broad daylight
Silk ties   to match their tongues
30 pieces of silver   for any who go along
There is nothing new under the sun

I rise early the next morning, leaving Ron snoring in our tent. I head for a stream someone mentioned the previous evening. Following a hint of a trail, dodging pine trees and thick underbrush, I locate the stream, gurgling softly; shallow and wide, sand and stones visible at the bottom. Pleasantly surprised, I spot Marvin. As I approach, he raises a cautioning finger. I freeze, looking about.

Birds are chirring and chittering; the chirping cacophonous, seemingly random. Yet as I listen, I detect patterns. I imagine if not a conversation, a sort of sonic dance; the birds holding court or at least commenting on all that is going on around them.

Marvin waves me over. I perch on a nearby boulder while he shifts his body, dangling his legs over a dirt bank as he faces the stream. On the other side, a meadow of tall grass and wildflowers. Recalling his talk at the museum, I ask if he has a favorite religion. Gazing across the meadow, he says he's come to believe *all* things are true. He turns to smile.

I shoot him a puzzled look.

Take the phrase, 'we are all the same,' he says, meaning human beings. This is true. We are all, in very many fundamental ways, *exactly* the same. Yet the opposite is also true. We are, each of us, uniquely ourselves. Like our fingerprints, no two exactly alike.

His smile widens.

Though diametrically opposed, both statements are equally true. It all depends on the context in which each is intended.

He again glances across the meadow.

So, God exists and God doesn't exist? I suggest.

Precisely. A part of me prefers not to use that word. It's a religious term. From one particular religion. What I call God is not arrived at only through religion. I for instance, found it through art. When Keats writes: Beauty is truth, truth beauty, I know exactly what he means. The laws of Beauty are the laws of Truth. And the laws of Truth are the laws of God; God in any religion.

An oriole swoops low, landing on the other side of the stream. We watch it peck at something in the grass. Soon it is joined by a companion. When both open their wings and fly away, Marvin glances up.

I'm talking about something that is infinite. Infinite meaning without limit. To say God is this super-intelligent consciousness gazing down at us, instructing us as what is right and what is wrong, is to limit God. We are saying God is *this*, as opposed to *that*. Thus, we confine it. To say God is *not* a super-intelligent consciousness, is also to confine it. I find it better not to say anything at all.

As we listen to the water lapping the side of the bank, he continues. I was in my late teens, early 20's, when I became vaguely aware of something. I knew it was there, but I couldn't exactly say what *IT* was. I was attending Boston University at the time. I recall at times leaving class, looking up over the trees and buildings, toward the sky. And I would see it. It wasn't the sky itself, or the clouds, or the sun bent toward the horizon. It was something else. And I would see it when I walked to campus in the morning. And at random times. I might look up from whatever I was doing and there it was. Yet there was no way I could point at it and say to someone: look at that—; do you see that—. I had no idea how to describe what I saw.

I found this disconcerting. See, I had come to college to become a writer—or more precisely, to see if I had the makings of becoming a writer. And yet here was something words could not capture. The very tools I had come to learn how to use were inadequate. I walked around in this funk for days. I seriously debated whether to give up becoming a writer. Part of me believed—naively maybe—that if I mastered how to use words, I would know the truth of things. Which was always important to me: to figure out what was true as opposed to what those around me were saying was true.

But then it hit me: symbolism. Symbolism, metaphor, parables, and stories. It is through these we can get around the limitations of ordinary language.

There was also something else happening at the time. I was becoming increasingly aware of how, whenever I was grappling with a problem, a personal problem or dilemma; something would provide me with the answer. It might be something someone said, something I overheard, or a piece of writing I'd stumble upon.

Once I was riding a bus and a page from a discarded newspaper landed right at my feet. Right at my feet. I picked it up. It was an op-ed page. I started reading this editorial, and lo and behold, there was the answer to something I had been wrestling with for days. Talk about synchronicity.

I had this growing sense that all the answers to all our problems were right in front of us, ready to reveal themselves. All we need do is step outside our egos, our preoccupations, and just look around, just listen; the answer would present itself.

He pauses for a long moment, me staring at him, he staring into the distance.

Over time, this awareness came to manifest in a number of ways, always at unexpected moments. I had dreams through which I knew something would happen before it happened. I had premonitions that proved dead on. I experienced these moments of astonishing clarity, sudden shifts in my perception which revealed the solution to a problem I had been wrestling with, sometimes for weeks. I had synchronistic encounters that steered me places which, once I arrived, I realized was exactly where I wanted—or more importantly—where I *needed* to be. At other times, a voice in my head would impart an insight or a tidbit of information which enabled me to successfully negotiate some situation I, up until that point, had been completely stymied by.

Always these various instances would manifest unexpectedly. Should I try to command or summon any of these instances on my own, I would fail miserably. I thus came to merely accept these instances as part of human experience. I had no explanation and sought none. They were merely bizarre occurrences I took as a natural part of being a living, breathing human being.

He pulls his knees to his chest and wraps his arms around them. A deer and its fawn appear on the far side of the meadow among the rabbitbrush and purple asters. They freeze just as Marvin ceases talking. They crane their heads in our direction. I wonder if they see us, maybe hear us. Perhaps they've picked up our scent. As they saunter off, he continues.

It wasn't until I stumbled upon the philosopher Plotinus. Ever hear of him? He lived some 200 years after Christ. Plotinus had a concept he called 'nous.' N-o-u-s. As I read him, I became acutely aware that Plotinus recognized the very same thing I had been aware of. It wasn't necessarily his concept, but something about his concept told me he and I recognized the same thing. I was certain of it.

He further made me aware that I had been viewing it—whatever *IT* was—as if out of the corner of my eye. I never thought to look at it head-on and ask, *what exactly is going on here?* I came to realize I had been seeing it in fragments, never entirely piecing it all together.

Plotinus noted the existence of the material world and the world of the spirit or soul. According to Plotinus, neither realm was subordinate to the other, but it was only through the spiritual realm one could access what he called *nous*. This mirrored my own experience. I did not access what I had been aware of through the material world. I always accessed it though another portal.

He glances over at me.

In college I wrote a paper on Franz Kafka's 'The Hunger Artist.' In my research, I came to understand Kafka's hunger artist could be interpreted as either a religious ascetic: someone who fasted for the sake of spiritual enlightenment; or as an artist—artists being people who forego material comfort for the sake of his/her art. I recognized I had stumbled upon my awareness of what Plotinus and I saw, through my pursuit of becoming an artist. So, it dawned on me: the two personality types most likely to stumble upon the awareness both Plotinus and I had, would be religious ascetics and artists as both down-play the material world.

After reading Plotinus, my brain was on fire. I put the book down and decided to take a long walk. Coincidentally—or synchronistically—I run into a couple of Jehovah Witnesses; an older woman with a warm and friendly disposition, and this very attractive Hispanic woman, perhaps in her early twenties, carrying an infant. The older woman did most of the conversing, trying to persuade me the end times were at hand and there was only one way to save my soul. I, in turn, tried to share all that was bubbling up inside me. As you might imagine, though cordial, our conversation went nowhere.

After they left, I began to think about Jesus. Jesus was the only religious ascetic I had any knowledge of. I considered myself an atheist at the time, but I had nonetheless taken the trouble to read the Bible cover to cover. Like I said, I had always been interested in learning the truth about things, so it seemed to me, you should read things that challenge your own belief system. As I pondered Jesus, I suddenly realized that should I substitute what Plotinus and I recognized, for what Jesus called 'God the Father,' everything Jesus said and stood for, made absolute perfect sense. I instantly understood why Jesus was so revered. And rightly so. I further understood that Christianity, despite its flaws, its hypocrisies and short-comings had been built on a very solid foundation. There had to be many, many others within that faith who recognized precisely what Jesus, Plotinus and I were aware of. Otherwise, the religion would not have survived, never mind thrived over the past two thousand years.

But the revelations did not end there. A short time later, I was visiting friends who took me to an art museum. This was in Philadelphia. There was a traveling exhibit of Hindu art on the main floor. I can still recall clearly staring at the first few paintings, reading the accompanying comments, and feeling something stir inside me. Within minutes, I was overtaken by the profound realization that what I and Jesus and Plotinus were aware of, the Hindus also recognized. They had devised an entirely different set of symbols to get at it, but it was the same awareness.

My initial shock was instantly followed by an *Of course!* I could have smacked myself in the head. It should have been the most obvious thing in the world. What Jesus, Plotinus and I were aware of was universal and ubiquitous. It would stand to reason the religious geniuses of the Hindu faith—the religious/spiritual geniuses of any faith and civilization—would recognize the precise thing Jesus, Plotinus and I were aware; that each culture would devise its own system of appropriate symbols to get at something that was ultimately ineffable. None could say exactly what it is. Each would be forced to describe what it is LIKE. Each would assign an image or series of images to get at a mystery nearly impossible to explain.

A breeze suddenly kicks up, shaking the leaves and bushes around us. Several magpies swoop across the sky. In the distance I see Andrew approaching on his tiny legs. Breakfast is about ready, he announces.

Marvin rises and brushes the seat of his pants as we follow Andrew back to camp.

Repeat, repeat,
repeat

IV

The previous evening, I got to know some members of the troupe. Rico is a history buff, having earned a BA from a community college outside of Boston. Boston is where they all reside. Jamal, in his late 40's, was a Jungian psychoanalyst though he had given up that profession in favor of what he called a more bohemian lifestyle. Harvey, the elder of the group, once studied to become a Jesuit priest, only doubts about God and a sex scandal cover-up at the religious university he attended, turned him in a different direction.

The troupe had been booked to perform in Denver at a place called The Temple of (Wo)Man. They, along with three guest speakers of national and international reputation, were to put on a presentation billed as The Theater of Self-Emancipation.

I had hoped to spend what remained of the afternoon hanging around Marvin, but by the time Ron and I pitched our tent, Marvin was not to be found. Gone on a long walk, someone told us. He does that, someone else added. I busied myself helping Rikki set up a folding table on which to stack paper plates, cups, napkins, and miscellaneous supplies. Then I helped chop vegetables while Ron helped collect firewood and Harvey marinated chicken wings and seasoned hamburger patties. Pete and Andrew brought out a cooler filled with wine, beer, water, and soft drinks. Marvin returned just as the first of the hamburgers and chicken were ready for consumption. We loaded our plates, Rico expounding on some ideas he had been mulling over, ideas related to the rise and decline of great civilizations.

He postulated that early in any great civilization's founding, influential citizens tended to display great discipline and moral fortitude, this being necessary first to survive, then to thrive. Thus, they arrive at a series of hard-earned, time-tested ideals which they adhere to faithfully. They in essence codify a few of the world's great truths which they then pass onto succeeding generations.

Andrew: Somewhat like this country's founders.

Rico: Exactly. They pass these ideals onto their children. And the children, being in direct contact with their parents, pretty much understand and embrace these truths. Only something changes with the grandkids.

The grandkids get to enjoy all the benefits of the new, thriving society, while never having gone through the trials and struggles their grandparents and great-grandparents had to endure in order to arrive at these truths. As such, the grandchildren fail to internalize the ideals with the same resonance and commitment as the grandparents, or even the parents.

Rikki: In other words, they take the ideals for granted.

Rico: Exactly. And this becomes even more true with the great-grandchildren and great-great-grandchildren and each successive generation. Until, over the decades, you have a society where the bulk of its citizens honor the founders, mouth the clichés, perform the rituals, yet don't truly embrace or fully appreciate what the founders stood for, and maybe died for.

Harvey: The same happens with religion. Look at how today, you have churches protecting pedophile priests when you'd think such behavior would be completely antithetical to everything the church is supposed to stand for.

Jamal: Something else happens.

Jamal paused from stirring the fire to add more wood to the flame.

As any empire gains solid footing, eventually—inevitably—the ultra-wealthy manage to gain control of the levers of power. When that happens, they begin instituting policies designed more toward increasing their wealth and power, over the health and well-being of the general population.

Harvey: The universal struggle of property versus people.

Jamal: After which, more and more on the lower rungs of society begin to struggle and suffer. And meanwhile the wealthy and powerful, not prone to concern themselves with the suffering of the masses, dig in their heels, ignoring the growing protests and atmosphere of mounting discontent.

Harvey: Which is probably what is happening today. Look how nothing meaningful is being done to address increasing homelessness. Or the housing crisis.

Rikki: Or rising food prices.

Harvey: Or rising food prices. People working multiple jobs and still barely able to make ends meet.

Pete: Not to mention addressing the almost daily mass shootings.

Jamal: That too.

Rikki: The top ten percent of the population owning more than 80 percent of the nation's wealth.

Rico: The bottom 50 percent owning barely one

percent. It's a scenario that happens throughout history. In most cultures. Take the Carnegies and the Rockefellers living high on the hog while the working poor were going on strike after strike, being beat back by local, state and sometimes even the federal government.

Harvey: And here we are again. Protest after protest while politicians in the pockets of the wealthy make all kinds of excuses to do nothing.

Jamal: Till the bubble bursts.

Rico: Till the bubble bursts.

Marvin: Yet all experience hath shown that mankind is more disposed to suffer while evils are sufferable. I imagine we're awhile away from any cataclysmic explosion.

Jamal: But then again, explosions tend to happen unexpectedly, out of nowhere.

Marvin: True.

Andrew: States of great tension eventually seek release. That's basic physics.

Earlier Andrew had made a remark that caught my attention. A casual joke really, but one that hinted the group wasn't camping just for the sake of camping. Rather they were hiding out for their own safety. I'd further overheard Jamal and Harvey discuss driving into Denver to prepare for their upcoming performance. The debate seemed to revolve around limiting who should go and whether it was feasible to not include Marvin. When they noticed me within earshot, they lowered their voices, changing the subject.

The dinner conversation drifted into lighter, more casual banter, and lots of laughter. Andrew in particular would toss out lighthearted absurdities and awful, groan-inducing puns. I sat near Marvin, probing him, learning what I could about his background. He was author of four self-published books: three of poetry and one of short fiction, his last book starting to gain traction. I was jotting down titles when he turned to Pete. Ready? he asked.

They both rose as Marvin carried their plates to the trash bag and the two left. Pete returned carrying bongos. Marvin hauled a thick notebook along with a sack filled with percussion instruments. Rikki meanwhile had cleared the folding table and Rico took requests for drinks. One by one the others scattered, Harvey returning with a guitar, Rikki with a violin and bow. Andrew came ladened with hand drums and a sack of wooden flutes.

Jamal fed more wood to the fire as everyone settled in.

Marvin flipped open his notebook, turning pages back and forth. Eventually, he settled on one and began to recite:

> *When blood is crushed purple by toes of over-confidence*
> *then a star will tumble in the west and the antichrist will*
> *shiver of goosebumps*

Rikki began playing violin, the spare notes long and drawn out, the effect both sweet and melancholy.

> *When children dress in black, with shaved heads*
> *and sheared ideals, automobiles will rumble, echo thunder*
> *but eardrums popping to spastic rhythms will not compute*

Harvey plucked his guitar while Andrew, grabbing a few instruments from the bag Marvin had brought, added stray percussive sounds: the tinkling of jingle bells, the shake of a tambourine, several taps on a wood-block.

Marvin continued:

> *There is a hollowness at the heart of unhappy. . .*
> *One listens to the boom and watches the slithering of the sea*
> *staring at the white scar of beach, thoughts swelling*
>   *like a bruise*
> *I wonder if I can ever forgive. . .*

Harvey strummed his guitar. Rikki tapped the side of her violin, locking in on the guitar's rhythm. Andrew began playing an African talking drum, squeezing its sides as he tapped the drumhead, the tones of the drum changing with his movements. Pete joined in on bongos, at first tentatively, but with growing confidence. Marvin grabbed a maraca, adding light touches as he continued to recite.

> *I revisit the fragments of my dark path*
> *walk beside the scampering sea*
> *listening to the wind whacking the palm fronds*
> *It called me through my innocence*
> *I didn't understand its syntax*

The effect was hypnotic, Marvin's words cryptic yet suggestive. He'd toss out a few lines which he'd leave open-ended, allowing the others to respond, Rikki on her violin, Harvey on guitar. Andrew, after Pete took over on percussion, tooted notes on a flute. Ron and I smiled at each other, tapping our feet, taking over the responsibility of feeding the fire.

Jamal then began to recite, lifting a few phrases from Marvin — 'toes of over-confidence,' 'the slithering sea,' 'swelling like a bruise'—interweaving them into what I assumed was an improvised narrative. When he trailed off, Rico launched into a parable about an aging Caesar seeking redemption for the sins he had perpetrated over those he ruled.

The campfire popped and crackled. The sky eventually darkened and the stars came out. One long jam would end and another begin. At times, someone would recite a lengthier narrative. Some full of social commentary, others with a more political or metaphysical bent. Several full of sly, dark humor as when Marvin recited a rhyming poem of Lucifer getting a manicure while complaining about a housing shortage in Heaven resulting in humans overpopulating

Hades, making his existence sheer hell.

Harvey proved fond of slipping in scripture, even reciting from the Sermon on the Mount. He'd also create musical refrains from a phrase someone might toss out, interspersing singing within their monologues. Rikki and Jamal would at times jump in to harmonize.

The moon, not quite full, hovered in the night sky rife with stars, the swirl of the Milky Way faintly visible. I gazed up, concluding I was experiencing something profound, even mystical.

Eventually everyone packed up their gear and headed to their tents. The hum of myriad creatures, crickets, frogs, and an owl mingled with the sparks of the dying fire. After dousing the fire, Ron and I crawled into our sleeping bags, exhausted though mentally energized. I lay with my head in my hands recalling my first sighting of Marvin and my unexplained impulse to follow him. And now this bizarre coincidence: encountering him again, here of all places. I lay convinced something cosmic was happening; maybe even divine. I slept fitfully, mildly resentful of Ron who insisted we continue our hike the next morning.

Man does not live
by bread alone

V

Nothing new under the sun
Man does not live by bread alone
Still the bellyaching almighty dollar groans
Quid pro quo   leading back to Rome
Caligula stepping out of the closet
Nero twiddling his thumbs
One playing Monopoly, *the other* Game of Thrones
Deception dons the judge's robe
We hold these truths to be self-evident
Power corrupts   and absolute power?
Ban books from libraries
Condemn universities and any
preferring to think for themselves
*   Ignorance is bliss*
Easy to dazzle with sleight-of-hand
Now you see it   Now you won't
There is nothing new under the sun

I am privy to one more discussion session before Ron and I move on. We had packed our gear and were ready to bid farewell when Jamal approached, Marvin a few steps behind. Jamal asks if they might join us for part of our hike, explaining they were planning a hike themselves.

So, if you don't mind, we'd like to tag along, Marvin adds.

Ron and I nod in the affirmative. Harvey, Rikki, and Pete appear wearing backpacks and toting water bottles. Rico and Andrew wish Ron and me well, stating they will remain to look after the camp.

At Ron's urging we decide to climb one of the nearby peaks. It would afford a panoramic view of everything around us, he suggests. And sure enough, when we stand at its summit, we enjoy the illusion of feeling the entire world below our feet.

While Ron, Rikki, Pete, and I gawk at the view, Harvey, Jamal, and Marvin cluster together, Harvey passing around sandwiches and baggies of celery and carrot sticks. A casual comment leads to a discussion on Taoism.

The way I conduct myself in the world is very Tao, Marvin offers matter-of-factly. He bites into a carrot stick and chews before continuing.

In college, while taking comparative religions, I noticed many Taoist doctrines were concepts I myself had been arriving at. Only the Chinese had arrived at them spiritually while I was arriving at them philosophically.

You're like me, Harvey cuts in. Growing up, I so wanted to believe in God. And for years I did. Or believed I did. I told myself I did. Mainly to appease my parents who were very devout. But deep down, I could never fully accept God up here.

He taps his head.

Jamal: There are four ways we experience our reality; at least in Jungian psychology. Four ways we interface with the world around us. Marvin, you remember discussing this.

Marvin nods.

Jamal: The two dominant ways are through either our feelings. . .or through our intellect. Some of us lean more toward thinking, understanding things rationally, while others go with whatever their emotions tell them. We utilize both, but we each tend to favor one over the other.

Marvin: The other two ways are through our five senses. . . or through our intuition. I had this roommate in college, Ted. Ted used to tease me because even though I had this very analytical mind and would, like Hamlet, weigh things over and over before making a decision, when it came to actually doing something, I would follow this impulse that wasn't necessarily the more logical thing to do.

Jamal: Your intuition.

Marvin: Exactly. And I have Jung to thank for making me aware of my intuitive nature. I'd heard the word, but never really thought about it until I read Jung. Once I became cognizant of it, I learned to cultivate my intuition—especially in my writing.

I learned, for instance, to let go of my stories and poems. I ceased to control whatever came out of my pen. Which is very Tao. I never focus on what I might be trying to say. I never intentionally advocate a particular point of view or force my writing to preach something I want others to believe.

I took part in this project years ago in which we were studying the merits of art therapy: visual arts, music, writing, dance, theater. One of our findings is that one can't help but express who one is. Everything we create is an expression of the person creating it. When you paint, for instance, the colors you gravitate toward, the lines you draw, are all expressions of whatever is going on inside you, particularly at the moment of creation. It can't be helped.

Thus, everything I write is an expression of who I am: all that I've experienced, all that I've read and thought, all that happens to be marinating inside me at the time I sit down to write. Who I am, is bound to manifest in whatever I create. Therefore, there is no need to control it.

Harvey: Same with our performances.

Marvin: Yes, exactly. We have an outline, a theme; a general idea of where we want to go. But then we let go and trust whatever unfolds naturally. Which is all very Tao.

Jamal: I recall you once saying you consider the *I-Ching* the most brilliant book you've ever read.

Marvin: I still do. That Confucius and the Chinese could figure out all they had figured out just astounds me.

The *I-Ching* is also called the *Book of Changes*, the Chinese understanding everything is always changing; the only constant is change. Though we in the West somewhat recognize this, we still have a tendency to think linearly—in terms of a beginning, middle and end. Remember Harvey's talk on how some Christians and Christian dominations cling to the idea of an end time; some kind of Rapture where the chosen rise up to live forever while all sinners are damned; when reality as we know it, stops.

Harvey: Which is ridiculous. Never going to happen.

Marvin: Not if you interpret the Rapture *literally*. The Ancient Chinese, on the other hand, recognize things are always changing, but the changes are cyclical. What comes around once, comes around again and again, and keeps coming around. One state naturally flowing into the next which then flows into the next, which flows into the next till eventually things come back to the beginning.

Jamal: There actually being no beginning. No beginning and no end.

Marvin: Right. The *I-Ching* uses what? – 64 hexagrams to chart different situations going from one state into the next. In the West for instance, when Jesus says, 'turn the other cheek,' some Christians will conclude: well, the Lord says I should turn the other cheek, so in every circumstance that's what I'll do. The Chinese would say no, wrong. Although turning the other cheek is a profound insight and a highly effective course of action, probably the best course of action in most cases—there will be situations when turning the other cheek will not net the desired result. Thus, in their hexagrams, although a major course of action or response is recommended, it offers minor adjustments or alternatives depending on the given circumstances.

Whereas in the West, we think of ourselves as machines made up of various parts that work in a particular way, the Chinese perspective sees humans as organic. We don't operate by the laws of mechanics. We operate by the laws of Nature; the same laws all other living entities operate by. We aren't constructed. We start as a seed which grows, transforms, and matures, changing every day. Eventually we reach full maturity, after which we begin our slow decline, as do all living things.

Marvin bites on a celery stick.

Many of the metaphors Lao Tzu uses in the *Tao Te Ching* stem from observations of Nature. Which doesn't surprise me—another thing I and the Chinese perspective share in common.

There are many paths to what we call God. Not just religion. I found what I call God through my pursuit of beauty. My theory is the laws of Beauty are the laws of Nature. We experience Beauty first in Nature. The beauty of sunrises and sunsets...of early spring when leaves begin to bud and flowers bloom....warm summer nights staring up at the stars...that silent hush in winter when the entire landscape is covered in snow. Then we try to duplicate that beauty in art—in music, painting, literature, in dance. The laws of Beauty are the laws of Nature are the laws of God.

To my mind, nowhere is the word of God more indelibly written than in Nature. For that reason, there are many who, failing to find God in religion—or in Beauty—find it in Nature. There is a reason we experience this universal sense of peace and well-being when we immerse ourselves in the natural world.

Still others find God through devoting their lives to relieving the suffering of others, in bettering the world and serving mankind; sacrificing one's own narrow self-interest to provide comfort to others; following the example Jesus set. In doing so, you tap into the human frailty and community that unites us all into one vast brotherhood.

Rikki: And sisterhood

Marvin: And sisterhood. Then there is a vast number of people who find God simply through Love. There becomes something in such a person's nature or through the course of their life experience that lead them to sincerely love everyone and everything in the same way they would wish themselves to be loved. In doing so, they wind up standing at the right hand of what the Biblical writers identified as God.

Harvey: Amen.

Marvin: Whatever you call it, it has an infinite number of ways to reach into the lives of each of us. After all, it is universal and ubiquitous. Always right in front of us—always reaching out, waiting for us to take notice.

Jamal: It also reaches out to different aspects of our individual personalities. Some through our intellect. Some through the heart. Others spiritually, intuitively, or artistically.

Marvin: That too, though recognizing God—or whatever you chose to call it—is rarely either/or. Most of us recognize it only to varying degrees. Say 75 to 80 percent. Maybe to 50 or 40 percent. Even the most misguided among us will have brief moments of connection.

How can you know when someone truly recognizes God? I ask.

That's the million-dollar question, Harvey smiles.

Marvin: For me, the best clue is how they treat and talk about their fellow human beings. That tells me all I need to know. I call it being God-centered. When one is God-centered, one recognizes that every act—especially those involving other people—has the potential of either hurting or healing. When one is God-centered, you always opt for healing.

A tingling shoots up my spine. Heat burns my cheeks. Momentarily I consider letting Ron continue our hike alone, me wanting to return to their camp and immerse myself in whatever insights I might learn from these men, especially Marvin. I make sure to exchange contact information, determined to rejoin them as soon as Ron and his family head back east.

During our hike, I had walked a spell with Pete and Rikki. We fell behind to smoke a joint. Pete mentioned earning his living fixing things—lawn mowers, leaf blowers, furnaces, electronic equipment, sound speakers. He was the troupe's sound and light engineer, brought on board through his friendship with Rikki. Rikki was a classically-trained musician who had taught music in public schools until, in her words, the oppressive bureaucratic nature of the education system had her throwing her hands up in disgust. She was the newest member of the ensemble. Their upcoming performance would be her first major appearance.

Nervous? I asked.

No, she replied. Only—

Only what?

She's worried, Pete stated.

Worried?

About the death threats.

Death threats?

Rikki nodded. The shooting at the Cultural Center . . .we don't know if it was related but. . .there have been these death threats. More and more lately.

You're kidding. Why?

Pete mentions a video that went viral.

I was later to view the video, a crude but hilarious recording someone had streamed live. In it, Rico is dressed as a witch, wearing a yellow wig, parodying the speech pattern of the President, speaking in absurdly hilarious hyperbole. Marvin inserts quick cryptic verses on Narcisus dry-humping his reflection in a mirror and the antichrist waving an upside-down Bible while mangling scripture. Harvey tosses in the four horsemen of the apocalypse, each a prominent politician currently embroiled in a sex or fraud scandal.

It's a witch hunt! Rico repeatedly proclaims. *Where's my broom? I'll sweep away this swamp. I know! I'll sweep it under this rug.*

As he rants, Harvey recites:

Double, double, toil and trouble
Fire burn and cauldron bubble,

the others humming 'The Battle Hymn to the Republic' in the background.

This dovetails into Marvin reciting a lengthy poem using common phrases from the Bible, the U.S. Constitution and the Declaration of Independence to rail against government corruption.

Pete: It really pissed some people off. . .

Rikki: Lots of people. . .especially supporters of you-know-who.

Pete: . . lots of hecklers on social media. This one group in particular.

Rikki: They re-posted the video with Rico, Marvin and Harvey being hanged and repeatedly stabbed, the words 'We're Coming After You' in dripping red letters.

Pete: The police suggested we lay low. They're supposed to increase security during the show.

Standing at the summit, listening to the others, I ponder the Second Coming. Not Christ returning in all His glory to signify the end times. Rather Christ coming back to be executed again. I consider what has just been said earlier regarding things happening once, coming around to happen again. And again.

As Harvey repacks their uneaten snacks, I flash on Jesus and his disciples consuming their last meal, even while telling myself not to be so melodramatic.

All men are endowed
by their Creator

VI

There is nothing new under the sun
All men are endowed by their creator
He that toileth
That fat furry cats   and belligerent muskrats
may soak up the sun
He that beggeth for bread
while Marie Antoinettes croon Let them eat cake
Do unto others before they know what hit them
Check and balances   unbalanced
*   and checked*
You reap what you sow
All men are endowed by their creator
Not the first time
Corruption grabbed hold of the handlebars
Steering the pursuit of happiness toward a precarious cliff
Justice with its hands in it pockets
while love of money   the root of it all
*   rearranges the Supreme Court's docket*
You can fool some of the people all of the time
(And sometimes that's just enough)
*   Not the first time*

After returning to Denver and bidding Ron and wife farewell, I contact Marvin. He informs me they are back in the city, staying in various homes provided by friends of the event. I offer to volunteer in any capacity the troupe may need me. Marvin suggests I join him and a few others for breakfast. Afterward, everyone will meet at The Temple of (Wo)Man to check out the performance space. When I arrive at the restaurant, Rico and Harvey are already seated.

Rico is staring up at a flat screen TV, the sound off, closed captions flashing along the bottom. A bombastic politician is asserting the U.S. is the greatest country in the world. The greatest country in the history of the world, he adds.

Rico guffaws. What a bunch of—. People who say that don't know a damn thing about history.

Catching me out of the corner of his eye, he greets me, as does Harvey. We exchange hellos as Harvey slides over so I can sit.

We're nothing but a bunch of Philistines, Rico continues, sipping his coffee, glancing around the restaurant. We're barely 250 years old, for Christ's sake. Rome lasted a thousand years. Ancient Greece over 600. We're infants by comparison. Arrogant little adolescents thinking we know everything.

Smiling my way, Harvey nods. You're right, he says. We've yet to produce a Plato or an Aristotle. A Homer, or a Dante.

Rico: A Shakespeare, Michelangelo, or Beethoven.

Harvey: A Jesus or a Buddha.

Rico: As far as I can see, this country has achieved only two things. For one, we can do whatever the hell we want with matter. We've figured out the laws of chemistry and physics. We can make bombs that can blow up the whole world. We can compress vast libraries into these tiny cell phones. We can build rockets that can travel to distant planets. We've brought the material world to its knees.

He sips his coffee.

And the second thing? I ask.

He again glances around the restaurant.

We have more creative ways to kill larger numbers of people than any other so-called civilization in the history of the world.

Harvey: We equate being the richest, most powerful country in the world with being the greatest.

Rico: Which is the mentality of Philistines.

Here's Marvin and Andrew, I say, pointing past Rico's head.

Andrew waves as he and Marvin approach. We exchange greetings as everyone settles in. I recap my travels with Ron through the Rocky Mountains. They recount their adventure camping. We order breakfast, the conversation shifting to their upcoming show.

Rico, I discover, is their costume designer. The plan is for each of them to assume a persona. Marvin is to be a prophet, a reluctant messiah as he puts it. Jamal is to dress as a U.S. senator: suit and tie, a small American flag pinned to his lapel, his cufflinks also American flags. Harvey will portray a Catholic priest while Rico will ride in as Don Quixote, Rikki his Poncho Sanchez.

The exception is Andrew who will wear a navy-blue T-shirt displaying a hydrogen atom and the formula $E=mc^2$ in large letters. He is to sit center stage surrounded by his drums and flutes, the others seeming to orbit around him.

I learn further Jamal plays electric bass and Rico synthesizers.

I inform Marvin I ordered two of his books.

He smiles and sips his tea. Hope you enjoy them, he says. Mainly all I do is experiment. One of my favorite quotes is from Einstein: *Genius is the ability to play*. That describes perfectly how I write. My great joy in writing is playing with language, experimenting with style and form.

Jokingly I ask if he considers himself a genius.

Taking a moment, he responds: I don't believe genius is something we are. Rather something we have. And we all have it. Some people are just better at tapping into it than others. Yeah, there's IQ genius, I guess—people born with an unusually high IQ. But there's another kind of genius.

I used to consider a couple of friends I performed with geniuses. They were amazing. Incredibly talented. Come to learn later, they were both bipolar. While in their manic stage, they managed to tap into something I found awe-inspiring. Audiences were blown away as well.

I do think I have a so-called genius for how language works. Which is to say how the mind internalizes and interprets language. I mainly use sense imagery, for instance. As opposed to abstract phrasing. Abstract language requires the mind to think. It engages the intellect and requires that intellect to analyze what is being expressed. This can weary the mind much faster than sensory imagery. Sensory and concrete imagery engage sensory memory. With sensory images, we picture or imagine what is being described: a bird soaring, a bell ringing, the smell and sizzle of bacon frying. We then draw associations which bypass intellectual analysis. The mind doesn't analyze, it associates. Thus, it doesn't tire as quickly.

My theory is the average listener can only handle about 20 minutes of poetry non-stop. After that, the mind tires, the brain loses concentration and seeks to wander. But with sensory imagery you can hold a person's attention much longer.

Plus, sense imagery has the added advantage that it *suggests* rather than states. Instead of telling someone what I want him or her to think, I paint pictures which allow them to decide for themselves what they think or feel about whatever I am describing. This makes them an active participant in the story—which I found is the secret to good storytelling: you provide the reader sensory details they themselves assemble into a cohesive narrative.

He sips his tea.

I also make heavy use of ambiguity. Ambiguity, in fact, is my secret weapon. I use wording and phrasing which suggest multiple things at the same time. Your average reader may only pick up on one of the potential connotations—but they'll gravitate toward the suggestion which best reflects their own personal experience.

Thus, they impose their own reality to whatever scenario I am presenting.

As Marvin takes a bite of French toast, Andrew excuses himself to use the restroom.

And if that's not enough, I lull them with the musicality of my language. My use of sounds devices—alliteration, assonance, rhyme, slant rhyme—as well as the cadence and varied rhythm of my phrasing. I chose phrasing as much for the sound as for the meaning. Although the average listener may not be consciously aware, each phrase, each image, flows easily into the next. Should one image not grab or register its implication, it is quickly followed by another and another such that the mind will hopefully find enough provocative imagery to remain fully engaged till the end of each poem. That's why—at least, that's why I believe—most audiences respond favorably to my work. Isn't that right, Jamal?

Damn right.

Jamal bids me a warm welcome and the others a good morning. You guys ready? he asks.

Marvin finishes his breakfast. When Andrew returns, we divvy up the check and leave.

Unlike the Museum and Cultural Center where I first saw Marvin speak, the Temple of (Wo)Man has nothing regal about it. It is a three-story structure made of wood in need of a fresh coat of paint. Perhaps once a group of separate apartments, it currently boasts a series of large rooms used as meeting, dining, and meditating spaces. The main floor has been converted into a narrow auditorium with a modest stage at one end. Backstage leads to stairs descending into a basement lounge with adjoining dressing rooms. Rikki and Pete are there to greet us along with a slight man, probably in his 50's, named Thomas Cavanaugh. Call me Tom, he insists, removing his spectacles and offering a toothy smile.

As he leads us back to the stage, he informs us a decent crowd is expected. There will be three guest speakers, he mentions: one to address the challenges of climate change, another to discuss human overpopulation, the third to talk about the human transformation necessary for our species to survive its current challenges. Half the tickets have been donated, he says, the other half nearly sold out.

Jamal, Harvey, and the others determine where each will set-up their instruments. They further discuss the still-to-be-completed backdrop Marvin will squat in front of. The idea is for it to look like the entry to a cave, Marvin seated at its entrance against what is to look like a large boulder. Under Rico's instructions, a volunteer artist will complete the backdrop that evening.

When the details are sorted out, Tom provides directions to a park where various organizers and volunteers are gathering for a mid-afternoon cook-out. And where, he adds, the troupe could hold the last of their 'infamous' (his term) consciousness-raising sessions before tomorrow night's performance.

At the park 50-70 people are gathered in various groups, the smell of grilled chicken, hot dogs, hamburgers, and sausage permeating the air. The troupe is greeted enthusiastically, their reputation apparently having preceded them. Some are anxious to shake their hands; others solicit a warm hug. I gather some are members of a steering committee, others from the Temple's Board of Directors. Still others are volunteers or family members of any of these groups. The bulk are elderly though bright-eyed, with lively spirits and intelligent faces. Most strike me as members of various liberal spiritual organizations or social activists.

As none of the troupe except Rikki and Pete are hungry, we partake in drinking wine coolers or beer,

Marvin and Harvey content to drink water. After those eating are well-fed, everyone gravitates toward a wide grassy knoll, its steep incline facing a flat area where chairs are arranged for members of the troupe. Andrew is seated in the middle, Marvin and Harvey on either side of him, Jamal and Rico on either side of them. Rikki, Pete, and I sit to one side along with Tom and a few other Temple officials.

Andrew stands, welcoming everyone and introducing the others. He acknowledges Tom and a few other officials as well as two of the three speakers slated to appear the following evening. He provides background on himself, mentioning he is a physicist by trade, having participated in several national and one international study on particle acceleration, his specialty being quantum physics.

He launches into a brief overview of Newtonian physics, mentioning thinkers like Copernicus and Newton who ushered in the age of what he calls classical science—the science he says we all studied in high school and at most universities. The guiding principle of Newtonian science, he states, is predictability. Once we isolate the major causes of any physical phenomenon, we can then predict subsequent occurrences with near or absolute certainty, certainty being the gold standard for labeling anything a 'scientific truth' (He adds air quotes). Ever since the Ancient Greeks, he continues, the goal was to break down matter into its absolute smallest components, the smallest component in Newtonian physics being the atom.

However, in studying the nature of this supposed smallest component, scientists found they could break the atom down even further, down to the sub-atomic level. Only in observing sub-atomic particles, scientists found they could no longer predict anything with absolute certainty. The best we could do is predict *probabilities*: what might *probably* happen, but could possibly *not* happen. Thus, the birth of quantum physics.

The interesting thing about measuring probabilities, he continues—the probability that this might happen or that might happen—depends on where one is standing. Are you standing at the beginning of a process and thus watching how an event unfolds? Or are you observing the end of the process where one of the several probabilities actually manifests? At the sub-atomic level, things happen too fast to observe both. Depending on where you are standing, you will observe a different event.

Now that might seem like some mambo-jumbo but the main point is: what you observe depends on where you are standing. Thus, you as the observer, influence the result—or at least how you perceive the result. Wherever you stand, whatever you perceive, influences what appears real to you. Welcome to Relativity.

Einstein theorized a beam of light will appear to travel differently should you stand at the source of that beam of light, as opposed to if you were to travel *on* that beam of light. Our realities are subjective depending on where we stand—or, in this case, where we sit.

What is more, in quantum physics, there is the realization that matter and energy are the same thing. $E = mc^2$ means that energy is equal to mass times c, c being the speed of light, in this case, squared. At the sub-atomic level, energy and mass are not separate: they are two aspects of the same thing.

The space-time continuum—I'm sure you've heard that term—the space-time continuum means space and time are the same thing. We – you and me – are three dimensional creatures: height, width, depth. We see and experience our reality in three dimensions. Only at the turn of the 20th century did time become considered a dimension. As three-dimensional creatures, all we experience of time is the here and now. We no longer experience what is past although we can remember it. Nor do we experience the future. We can contemplate its numerous possibilities (sound familiar?), but we can't experience the future. We only experience the here and now.

Many of you have heard the phrase: Be Here Now, a concept embraced in Eastern thought; the same concept quantum physics has arrived at. Were we traveling at the speed of light, what now takes us days, if not months to experience, we would be experiencing in the blink of an eye. Time seems stretched to us, but traveling at the speed of light—the speed of light squared—all things would be happening simultaneously. Only as three-dimensional, slow-moving creatures, we don't experience it that way. Welcome, as I said, to Relativity.

The space-time continuum states that space and time are actually the same thing; two different forms of the same thing. In their own way, Eastern and Chinese thought have millennia ago, arrived at this very same conclusion. Body and soul are not separate, they are two forms of the same thing. Matter and energy, matter and consciousness, are not separate: they are two manifestations of the same thing.

Those deadlocked in Newtonian physics sometimes assume matter is all there is. Energy moves matters, but it is all matter in motion, nothing else. In Eastern thought, they postulate the very opposite: it all begins with *consciousness*, consciousness being a form of energy. It is consciousness that converts all we encounter *into* matter. Consciousness creates the universe, just as we, each of us, in a very real sense, create our own realities.

I could go on. Much of what is being discovered, or theorized, in quantum physics—the possibility of multiple universes, the existence and nature of black holes—have corresponding theories in Eastern and Chinese thought. The Chinese concept of yin and yang: opposites in which one could not exist without the other because each is an essential component of the same process. In quantum physics, sub-atomic particles go through a perpetual process of creation, annihilation, and transformation—not that different from the Hindu concept of creation, destruction, rebirth. Science is the study of our physical reality. Religion and philosophy are the study of our metaphysical reality; two manifestations of the same reality. In Eastern religion and philosophy, the world of matter is a relative world. It is an illusionary world; not illusionary in that it doesn't exist, but in that we never see it as it fully is, only as wherever we are standing allows us to see it. Thus, the quest of Buddhists and Hindus is to see beyond this veil.

At this point a full discussion opens, people raising hands, asking questions, and offering comments. Marvin expounds on an idea he'd mentioned at the Museum: the Hindu concept of human existence being an eternal drama or dance. Andrew observes this is not unlike how some quantum physicists describe the behavior of sub-atomic particles and waves—as a dance.

Marvin: According to Hindu cosmology. . .there is a period of peace and stability, a relatively lengthy period. . .followed by another lengthy though shorter period where instability manifests—though things are still relatively good. This is followed by a period where the forces of light and the forces of dark are relatively equal. One is not sure which way things will go. Then, should things go seriously awry, comes the shortest period of all, when the negative triumphs and wreaks havoc and destruction. Think of World War II: six years of sheer devastation before everything is again righted.

Rico: Or our Civil War: four years of bitter fighting—the culmination of decades of tension between abolitionists and slave owners.

Marvin: Then afterward, we again return to a period of peace and stability. During which we determine as best we can what caused the instability and take steps to ensure such a situation never occurs again.

Harvey: Until, decades later, it of course does. In some new, unanticipated way.

Marvin: But in the meantime, we construct a noticeably better community and humanity as a whole advances. That is the eternal dance. The polarization in this country today, like that leading up to our Civil War—the tension between peoples throughout history—is our human dance, our way of creating, *transforming* if you will, our reality.

Rico: Another example: the tension in the 18th Century Europe which led to the American and French revolutions, resulting in democratic governments taking root in Europe and America, and now around the globe.

Jamal: Or the Industrial Revolution, creating tension between capitalism and socialist ideas. For some two centuries now, we as a species, have been juggling to balance the needs of the general population with the sadly all-too-human propensity toward selfish greed. A me-versus-them mentality. Survival of the fittest. My self-interest vs. the common good. Out of this struggle we are creating our current reality.

Marvin: Our current dance. Hopefully, like the end of a Bollywood movie, there will be reconciliation. A state where balance and harmony are once again restored.

Rico: Either that or we could end up destroying ourselves.

Marvin: In which case, those who survive will take to heart the lessons learned and hopefully lead humanity in a new, more positive direction.

Jamal: Over and over, ad infinitum.

Marvin: Sadly, states of harmony and balance cannot sustain themselves permanently. Yet, if each of us influences, in effect *creates*, our collective reality, the question for each of us here—and humanity as a whole—is which one shall we as individuals work toward: the negative or the positive? The selfish or the communal? We are, according to Hinduism, all manifestations of God and that is our eternal dance.

More questions and comments follow, Tom Cavanaugh finally standing to end the session. He thanks the troupe as well as everyone for coming. When the applause dies away, he encourages those who haven't already purchased tickets to do so. While some disperse, Marvin and the others are surrounded by people wishing to thank them or make last minute comments.

Recalling the death threats, I stand back, watching in particular those who approach Marvin. I scan the crowd for anyone who might appear suspicious. I make note of anyone standing in the periphery, looking on as I am. I see nothing suspicious. I spot two patrol cars parked a slight distance away. One has been there since we arrived. I breathe easy.

Happy there was no unpleasant incident, I look forward to tomorrow's culminating event. I drive home debating what I will do when the troupe leaves. Is all I have been learning, all I still could be learning, worth picking up and relocating to Boston for? I weigh the pros and cons, leaving any final decision in limbo.

The martyr once again
climbs his cross

VII

Not the first time
In this land   or any other
Ask Victoria, ask Lord Eden, ask Jesus
The martyr once again climbs his cross
Bleeding   truth to power
Sacrificed for other men's sins
Those who failed to learn from history condemned
There is nothing new under the sun
Now is the time for all good men
To come to the aid of their country once again
These be the times   that try men's souls
You can fool some of the people
*   but you can never fool them all*
Now is the time for all good men
all good women and children of pure hearts
to come to the aid of our forefathers
*   who art in Heaven*
having brought forth on this continent
a new nation of the people, by the people, for the people
in order to form a more perfect union
The arc of the moral universe though long
Bends always towards Justice, never Just Us
Power corrupts and absolute power inevitably
*   undermines*
our Father who art in Heaven
Man does not live by bread alone

While searching for the video of Rico dressed as a witch, I had stumbled upon another video, apparently an excerpt from a panel discussion. Marvin is seated at a long table, other speakers to his left and right. Behind him is a banner, the top line obscured, the bottom line reading: 'Stories & Storytelling.' The video cuts in abruptly during dwindling applause, apparently for a previous speaker. The camera zeroes in on Marvin.

We become the stories we tell ourselves, he begins, glancing around the room, shifting his chair to accommodate the microphone.

We tell ourselves these stories. In books, in movies, on TV, around the water cooler. Certain stories we tell repeatedly. So repeatedly, we come to believe the stories as true. Believing them true, we shape our lives accordingly. We cease to even question the validity of such beliefs. We fail to realize these beliefs are based on fictions we have been telling ourselves.

In the 50's and 60's, when I was coming up, the dominant culture told itself the story of Black people, people of my skin color, being inferior to white people; a story it had been telling itself for generations. So ingrained was this belief, no one had to tell me I was inferior. It was something I simply understood. I merely breathed it in like oxygen. I accepted it as an unquestioned fact—as did everyone around me, Black and white.

I was 16 when I saw through this fiction. In a flash of insight, I realized I was not innately inferior to white people due to my skin color or the blood that ran through my veins. I recognized my situation as what I called 'an accident of history.' I happened to be born at a time, within a culture, where the white race was on top and Blacks at the bottom. I speculated there were probably cultures in other historical periods where Blacks were on top and whites at the bottom. And there could very well be future times, countries, and cultures where the table might again be turned.

At that time, I concluded this story the dominant culture was telling itself—of whites being innately superior to Blacks—served two purposes for the white race. One, it allowed white people to elevate themselves in their own minds. There is no easier way for a person or a people to elevate themselves than to have someone to look down on. Black people served this function for the white race.

I further recognized the story created a near self-fulfilling prophecy. By convincing Black people we were inferior, we would be less inclined to make something of ourselves. Why reached for the stars when you are pre-destined to fall short? Thus, the dominant race had created a situation in which, at least on the surface, Blacks *did* appear inferior to their white counterparts. Our apparent inferiority was a by-product of the racial superiority story the dominant culture chose to tell itself. . .and us.

Growing up, I was fond of TV westerns. In these westerns, the American Indian was often portrayed as a hostile enemy, forever attacking wagon trains and killing decent white people; people on their way to forge a better life. Today, we tell ourselves a different story. We acknowledge what was done to the American Indian was wrong; that this nation fell well short of its democratic, Christian, and humanitarian ideals. We acknowledge we owe the Native American a deep apology. Stories can and do change. But any particular story we repeatedly tell ourselves inevitably comes to dictate our beliefs and as a consequence, our behavior. We should be cognizant and careful of the stories we choose to repeat.

There is another story we tell ourselves repeatedly. We tell it so consistently and so persistently, we have ceased to question its validity. As far as most citizens in this culture are concerned, it is an indisputable fact. Yet, a close examination will reveal it a mere fiction, a fiction we have convinced ourselves is true. I speak here of the story of Good vs. Evil.

Originating with the apocryphal literature of Judaism and gaining solid footing in this country's dominant religion and subsequent literature, the Good vs. Evil myth is currently trumpeted *ad nauseam* in our movies and popular fiction, in our daily disputes and in our way of thinking. Few would question the assumption that there exist these two forces, one called Good, the other Evil. According to the myth, these two forces are perpetually at war with each other. The forces for Good must be forever vigilant for Evil and its proponents, its Darth Vaders, are forever plotting and scheming to rule over us, to oppress all that is innocent, decent, and good. Add to the myth an impending apocalypse, a time projected in the always not-too-distant future when these two forces will clash in one final cataclysmic battle.

But there is a fundamental flaw in this myth: people never see *themselves* as evil. We only see *other people* as evil. Evil is what we call someone else, never ourselves.

The Ku Klux Klan, when it was lynching, castrating, and burning black bodies dangling from trees, cutting off body parts to keep as souvenirs, did not view themselves or their actions as evil. They viewed the possibility of Black men having sex with white women as evil. They viewed Black people being treated on equal par with whites as evil. Thus, to rid the South of *these* evils, the Klan resorted to lynching and terrorizing Black people. Acts which we today consider the epitome of evil, they found perfectly appropriate.

The same was true of Nazi Germany. The Nazis did not view themselves as evil. They viewed what they called the Jewish Conspiracy as evil. To rid the world of the evil that was the Jew, they came up with the Final Solution. Perfectly logical, given the story they were telling themselves.

This country did the same with the American Indian. We systematically stole this entire land from the people who rightfully owned it. Yet, every time they stood up to defend what was rightfully theirs, we labeled them evil savages, giving us the right to hunt them down like dogs and massacre their women and children along the way—all the while believing ourselves *Good* and them *Evil*.

We do this now with the people in the Middle East. We brand them evil, giving us the right to bomb or assassinate any of them as we see fit. Were the tables turned and they were bombing and assassinating us, we would consider their behavior the very height of Evil. More often than not, *evil is what we call someone else to justify doing evil to them*. The history of human persecution is overflowing with instances of one people calling another people evil so as to justify horrendous acts of slaughter and oppression: the Inquisitions, witch burnings, the Holocaust, the current war in Gaza, to name only a few.

The Good vs. Evil myth is a paradigm. It is a way of looking at the world or a given situation. But it is never as the world *is*. The world—our reality, our experience of being in the world—is always far more complex than our limited human understanding of it. There will be situations in which the Good vs. Evil paradigm may prove appropriate. But when applied to situations where it is inappropriate—which is most cases—the result is nearly always horrific, senseless slaughter and suffering.

There is a second, perhaps more insidious, flaw in the Good vs. Evil paradigm: *such a view necessitates an adversary*. When one subscribes unquestioningly to the Good and Evil Myth, one will need an enemy to validate one's world view. And where there is no enemy, we will create one.

In this nation's near 250 year history, most of our adversaries were created by our own attitudes and subsequent actions. The American Indian, Iran, Cuba, North Korea to name but a few. In each case, it was the U.S. who threw the first stone. In each case, we resorted to calling *them* evil to deflect our own responsibility in—if not causing the conflict—exacerbating it.

Without an enemy, we fight amongst ourselves. And those battles become very bitter and personal. Witness our current politics. But give us a common enemy, someone we can mutually hate, ideally fear, and we put aside our differences and join forces to annihilate that enemy. For some people, having an enemy gives purpose to their otherwise mundane lives. At no time will they feel more invigorated, more alive, than when confronted with a formidable foe in a life-or-death existential struggle.

We become the stories we tell ourselves. Thanks to the popularity of the Star Wars epic in the late 70's, we have had at least one, if not two, generations breastfed a constant diet of Good vs. Evil blockbusters. Add to this the Lord of Ring trilogy and countless vigilante and action/adventure movies in which a 'selfless' hero (usually white American male) sets out to combat some great evil injustice. Add further the recent fad of superhero movies feeding still younger generations a steady barrage of good vs. evil scenarios. The Good vs. Evil myth within our popular culture is currently on steroids.

Of particular note in these stories is the evildoer nearly always doing evil purely for evil's sake. Most humans are driven to transgress, to commit crimes, and even horrendous acts out of some personal or aggravating situation that drive them to eventually commit so-called evil acts. Not so these celluloid evildoers. They are innately evil, doing evil for evil's sake. The only way to defeat these cinematic bad guys—at least as far as your average screenwriter and director are concerned—is to blow these evildoers to smithereens. We no longer bother to capture and arrest these villains, then put them on trial. No, we annihilate them in cataclysmic, over-the-top, explosive final showdowns, applauding and patting our heroes on the back for exterminating such insidious vermin.

Our current obsession with the Good vs. Evil paradigm does not bode well for our future as a culture. Is it any wonder there are pockets of our population susceptible to all sorts of conspiracy theories, theories similar to the one the Nazi's used to hoodwink 1930's Germany? We become the stories we tell ourselves. Is it any wonder there are those bent on accumulating massive stores of military equipment in anticipation of an impending Armageddon with some government or deep state entity waiting in the sinister wings ready to pounce? As long as we inundate ourselves with an endless stream of good vs. evil stories, we will convince ourselves the threat of looming Evil is real, rather than something we project onto those we don't like.

There are of course other paradigms, other potential stories, our culture might gravitate towards. The Ancient Greeks, and after them the Romans, told very different stories. Stories not based on good vs. evil but based on tragic character flaws—the ultimate goal being to restore balance; not one side annihilating the other, but opposite sides finding common good.

It is important to note: no paradigm or story is the way the world *is*. No paradigm is the correct one and thus all others wrong. They are only different ways to look at the world and our experience within it. Each affords the ability to look at a given situation in a slightly—sometimes drastically—different way. Each has the potential to offer an insight or course of action another paradigm might miss.

The Ancient Greek paradigm is but one of many found at the core of humanity's past and present religions. The philosopher Alan Watts points out Western thought being locked into the concept of what he calls the 'ceramic model.' This is to say, in the West, we conceive the universe as something made, something created—much like a potter might create a bowl or a carpenter a chair. Thus, we view our world and ourselves as machines made up of various parts. We assume in understanding the various parts, we can ultimately understand the total machine—the machine that is us.

By contrast, the Asian perspective views the universe and ourselves as *organic*. We are not machines operating by the laws of mechanics but rather living matter operating by the same laws as all other living matter. We are not constructed. Rather we start as a seed which continually grows, changes, evolves. We blossom and bloom, cast our scent, spread our seed, then pass on, our rotting frames food and fuel for subsequent life.

Neither paradigm is necessarily the correct paradigm. Each affords a different insight into human experience. The East Indian perspective offers a still different paradigm; a different story which for brevity's sake, I will not explore here, but one which offers still different insights into our common human experience. The Western mechanical perspective is prone to argue one perspective must be right and thus the others mistaken. Right vs. wrong; good vs. evil. The Ancient Greeks would argue, each perspective holds its own merit. Rather than embrace one and cast the others aside, the Greeks would search for a balance, a golden mean between competing points of view.

As with the story of racial superiority, as with the story we told ourselves about the American Indian, we have the ability to change the story. We owe it to future generations and the health of our culture to extricate ourselves from our unquestioned embrace of the Good vs. Evil paradigm.

To veer away from simplistic Good vs. Evil scenarios will require years of deliberate, conscious effort. Total elimination is unrealistic, even unnecessary. Ratings and the necessity to tell engaging, conflict-driven stories, combined with the hackneyed skills of your average storyteller, all but ensures the worn-out cliché of Good vs. Evil will remain a staple of our entertainment diet. There is also validity and relevance to the Good vs. Evil myth. It contains valuable moral lessons regarding the very real and ever-present struggle between negative and positive forces, a struggle no society can afford to lose sight of. It is not the story itself, but the over-proliferation of the story that is unhealthy. That over-proliferation leads to our unquestioned embrace of a myth that all but guarantees we will be perpetually at each other's—or someone else's—throat.

We become the stories we tell ourselves. It is up to us, to our storytellers, to get beyond the narrow perimeters of Good vs. Evil. We are free to gravitate toward whichever paradigms offer the greater insights into any given situation. Free to gravitate to the paradigm that gets us closest to our collective goals. If perpetual war and conflict is the goal, we can stick to the Good vs. Evil myth. The myth all but ensures we will always have conflict, that we will perpetually seek out new adversaries to hurl our contempt at so as to elevate ourselves in our own minds. If the goal, however, is to reduce war and conflict, both with our self-created enemies and with ourselves—if the goal is to forge a greater sense of brotherhood among the varying peoples of the world, then our writers and storytellers, our directors, film, and TV producers would do us a great service by gravitating away from Good vs. Evil towards a very different story. We become the stories we tell ourselves. What we ultimately become, is in large measure, up to them. And up to us.

Marvin sat back, pushing the microphone toward the next speaker.

As applause erupted the video abruptly ended.

What you would have them do
unto you

VIII

Man does not live by bread alone
But in doing unto others
What you would have them do unto you
Now is the time for all good men to ask
  What would   LOVE   do?
    A Jesus by any other name
(And just who do the proponents of
Hate thy neighbor who does not think or act as you serve?)
Lucifer slips another log on the flame
Now is the time for all good men
To come to the aid of their heart's conscience:
The soul that knows   the TRUE root   of it all
    is how we choose to treat one another
Not who next we can beat down
(First, they came for immigrants,
for the woke, those of Arab descent, transgender youth
How long before they come for you?)
        divide and conquer

The morning of the performance, I swing by where Rico and Harvey are staying. While they load their equipment in Harvey's Datsun, I pile their costumes into my Toyota. We are first to arrive at the Temple of (Wo)Man. Rico and Harvey carry their equipment on stage while I lug the costumes to the basement dressing rooms. A bit later I assist Pete, plugging in cables and adjusting overhead lights. The others filter in, me making myself useful where I can. During a lull, several of us lounge about in the basement where Andrew and Rikki take lunch orders. Tom Cavanaugh, representing the Temple, offers to cover the cost. At one point, the culture wars is mentioned, Jamal hissing, calling the entire debate verbal sleight-of-hand.

Marvin agrees.

I remember watching this televised broadcast on

the culture wars, he says. I believe the actor Charlton Heston was the speaker. As I listened, my jaw dropped. I recognized immediately Heston was using the word 'war' metaphorically. There was no actual war going on. But by using the word 'war,' he was implying the other side was the enemy. In a war, you face an enemy out to suppress or destroy you, and the most natural response to someone out to destroy you, is to destroy them first.

Heston could have just as easily called it a 'debate': a cultural debate; debate also being a metaphor. But in a debate, two sides gather in a spirit of mutual respect and each presents his or her best argument, leaving it to the judges or the audience to decide which argument holds the most merit.

But no, he did not use debate; he used war. Whether consciously or subconsciously—probably both—Heston and his speech writer were *choosing* to cast their opponents as enemies; not good people who happen to hold a different opinion, but as an enemy out to destroy them unless they destroy that enemy first.

Jamal: A good example of what Andrew was talking about yesterday.

Harvey: How do you mean?

Jamal: Where we stand when viewing an event determines how we interpret that event. And how we interpret that event influences the outcome.

Marvin: Heston and his followers were convincing themselves to despise the opposing side; to view their opponents with contempt.

Jamal: Fast forward to today. The open contempt with which the political right view those on the left.

Harvey: And vice versa. When one side casts contempt on another, the other side is sure to respond in kind—if only as self-defense.

The discussion is interrupted by Rikki and Andrew

returning with lunch. As we divvy up who ordered what, the conversation shifts to art, Jamal noting the crucial role art plays in all human cultures.

Andrew, ever the physicist, queries the others as to why they think that is.

Rico posits art unites us. We see our own world resonate in the works other artists create.

It helps us realize none of us are alone, Rikki adds. We recognize our own thoughts and feelings; that others have experienced what we ourselves have gone through.

That's because we share the same reality, Marvin inserts. Though we experience it in different ways, it's the same reality—our common human experience. Art reveals the universal.

Art also plays a psychological role in the development of healthy individuals, Jamal offers. I have a hard time imagining anyone being a fully healthy and emotionally well-balanced individual without some sort of creative outlet. Even if it's cooking or macramé or building model airplanes.

Creative expression is not only good for the soul, but doubly-so for the emotionally troubled. It is a safe way to get what is going on internally, out—out on paper, out on canvas, into a song. Getting it out is a vital first step in confronting our inner demons. In a very real sense, art acts as a form of self-therapy.

Harvey: Not to mention the role it plays in passing along life's eternal truths, even down through the ages. In that sense, art functions very much like the world's great religions—without the dogma.

Marvin: In 10th grade I had this history teacher, Mr. McElwain. We spent the first several weeks studying Ancient Greece. I remember him saying, if we remember only one thing about Ancient Greece, we should remember 'Perfection.' It took years for me to figure out why he said that, but eventually I understood.

There is something about getting something perfect. And it can be about anything. Fixing a car. Cooking a meal. Organizing a party. Have you ever organized a party and handled every detail just right? Everything falls into place smoothly such that for days afterward, people are telling you what a great time they had?

Rikki: But isn't perfection subjective? Who determines when something is perfect?

Marvin: Don't think of it as perfection. Think of it as doing something to the best of your ability. It's not about getting something perfect; it's about *striving* to get it perfect. There is a kind of beauty when things fall into place just right. Something the Ancient Greeks had figured out in spades.

Rico: As did the Romans. And Florence during the Italian Renaissance.

Marvin: The Greeks had their act together in ways I think we today are lacking. In Greek mythology, you had a council of gods and goddesses. Things worked best when there was a consensus among the gods. Things go awry when one of the gods or goddesses feels offended or ignored.

Rico: Hence the concept of Democracy.

Marvin: Exactly. It wasn't about one side being right or the person at the top telling everyone below what to do. It wasn't about Zeus imposing his will for everyone else to follow. Each deity represented a different aspect of our multi-faceted reality—different value systems, different personality interests, each deserving a seat at the table; each perspective being honored.

The gods and goddesses were metaphors used to examine the underlying truths that govern human experience. In *The Odyssey*, when Athena visits Odysseus disguised as this person or that, that's a poetic way of stating

Odysseus was visited by wisdom. Poetic language is far more powerful, and more nuanced, than language limited by concrete thinking. When Moses parts the Red Sea, that's the author using hyperbole: purposely over-exaggerating something to drive home a point.

Harvey: Still, there *are* many who need to believe Moses literally parted the Red Sea; who need to believe David literally slew Goliath with only a rock and a slingshot.

Marvin: Which I won't quarrel with.

I remember once visiting this friend. When we were kids, Jake was always getting into trouble. Later he spent time in prison. After he got out, he married a devout Seventh Day Adventist; considered himself a born-again Christian. He confided in me having realized he was in essence a good person. Only he had this destructive tendency of follow his heart rather than his head, as he put it. This struck me at the time because I had just reached the very opposite conclusion about myself. I tended to follow my head instead of my heart.

But it made perfect sense he would gravitate to a take on Christianity which restricted his behavior; that demanded a strict set of do's and don'ts. A belief system that would hold in check his tendency to follow his more destructive impulses.

I, on the other hand, gravitated toward an understanding that freed me to do absolutely anything I wanted.

Anything? I challenge.

Anything, Marvin insists. It is not in my moral nature to hurt another human being. It is not in my nature to put my needs above anyone else's. I would never intentionally harm another soul, human or animal. Should I inadvertently harm someone, I would immediately make amends in every way I could. That leaves me free to do absolutely whatever I want because I will never purposely do any harm.

Harvey: The truth shall set you free.

Marvin: There *are* those who need to believe in Hell. Who need to fear eternal damnation should they transgress God's laws. They need to fear God's retribution so as to keep their destructive behaviors in check. Until they figure out another way to be. Which ultimately is just a mind shift, a simple attitude adjustment.

I *know* Hell doesn't exist. At least not as a place we go after we die. For me, hell is a condition we create for ourselves and those around us, here on earth, by the choices we make. My childhood was Hell. It was Hell partly because of how the dominant society chose to treat people of my skin color. It was Hell partly because of the way people of my skin color chose to treat one another as a consequence of how we were being treated by the dominant society. It was Hell because of a series of poor decisions my mother, as my sole guardian, made. And it was Hell partly because of decisions I made.

Even though I was a child and presumably innocent, I nevertheless made decisions. When they were good decisions, I benefited from them. When they were poor decisions, either I or someone else suffered from them. Once I figured that out, I made a point to make wiser decisions and the Hell that was my childhood gradually—rather quickly, actually—dissipated.

Harvey: The truth shall set you free.

Do you believe the Bible is the word of God? I ask.

Marvin pauses. I do and I don't, remember. I believe all things are true—given their context. If you mean that statement figuratively, I accept it wholeheartedly. Yes, the Bible *is* the Word of God. Each religion must have what I call a primary source: a source all believers can go to should there be any dispute over that religion's fundamental teachings.

It is inevitable that over time, there will come

these charismatic leaders who will put a new spin on the old traditions and teachings—some of which may stray drastically from what the founder and early disciples intended. When that happens, you need to go back to the primary source to settle any dispute. It is essential for Christians to insist the Bible is sacred; in effect, the Word of God. And for Muslims to insist the Quran sacred.

On the other hand, on a literal level, the Bible is a collection of writings written by various people over hundreds of years, many with varying understandings of what they each call God.

Harvey: Not just that. Those writings were collected and canonized by groups of priests who selected from the various writings available to them, excluding others. God both in the Old and New Testaments are God as seen through the lens of those religious scholars.

Marvin: The God in the Psalms is a God who rewards you if you are faithful, but punishes you when you stray. The God in Job inflicts suffering even if you are faithful. There is a section in Job which lists various ways God reveals Himself to us. One of those ways *is* through our suffering. That is a very different God than in Psalms who promises if you are good and faithful He will protect you from all harm and shower you with blessings.

Harvey: Or perhaps they are two sides of the same God.

Marvin: Which is a valid argument. It is not either/or, but both. In either case, the God I initially experienced is the God who revealed Himself through my suffering. As I said, my childhood was hell. But once I figured out the source of that hell, I was able to transcend my condition and, metaphorically speaking, re-enter the Garden of Eden.

Andrew: You two are far more tolerant than I am. I can't abide by denominations that gravitate toward a God who chooses favorites; who has a chosen people and thus rejects others as lesser.

Marvin: I hear you. Such an interpretation means these Christians must always have an Other, an enemy to keep their faithful toeing the line; some group they must always lash out against. Whether it be secular humanists, new agers, atheists, liberals, gay and lesbians, Christians of a different stripe. . .Muslims. These Christians must always have some group they view as offending God and thus deserving contempt if not annihilation.

Jamal: So long as that take on God persists, there will never be social tranquility.

Rico: There will never be world peace.

Marvin: I often remind myself that in the history of the great religions, Christianity and Islam are relative newcomers. Buddha, Confucius, and Lao Tzu were some 500 years before Christ; Hinduism well before that. Christianity and Islam are babes by comparison.

Now Judaism. . .

Marvin pauses, raising a finger.

Most of what I know of Judaism comes from reading the Old Testament. But I strongly suspect there is far more to that tradition than I currently comprehend.

I attended this memorial for the father of a close friend. Jewish. As I listened to the officiant—not sure if he was a rabbi or what—I recognized he was aware of the very same thing I identify as God. It was the first time I had encountered a *living* human being with the same awareness of God I had. Imagine my surprise. I had encountered it with philosophers and religious thinkers, even a few writers and poets, but never with a living person. I sat there amazed.

The other thing I will say about Judaism, is they produce great atheists.

You're laughing, but I'm serious. My entire life, I've

found myself admiring Jewish people. Not necessarily those practicing Judaism, but those who seemed more secular. I found them wonderful, caring, enlightened human beings. Dostoevsky points out how oftentimes the atheist is far closer to God than many so-called 'believers.' Other writers and religious thinkers have observed the same thing; that there is often a three-step process to fully recognizing God.

First, you embrace the lessons and legends you are taught as a child. Everyone around is telling you it's true so you accept it all at face value, without question. And many, many Christians never get beyond that elementary level of understanding. They believe because they are told to believe. But there are those who see a wide discrepancy between what is said and how the world actually is. They come to doubt. Especially given the blatant hypocrisy many die-hard Christians tend to exhibit. So, they reject God and develop their own set of beliefs based on the truths they hone from personal experience. If they are honest and sincere in their pursuit of separating truth from the lies and illusions people tell themselves, they arrive at a personal morality and way of being in the world that is far closer to God's will than many a card-carrying Christian. Whether they recognize it or not, they are firmly seated in the lap of God.

Then, for some, as in my case, the light bulb comes on. I realized God was not what I initially imagined growing up, but something else—something nonetheless very real; something which metaphorically *could* be described as a benevolent father gazing down on us from some unseeable height.

My last year of college I had these friends I would hang out with. At one point, I came to recognize they all shared several things in common.

First, they were all raised Catholic. They had

attended Catholic school, but had come to completely reject Catholicism. They had nothing nice to say about nuns or the Catholic faith.

Second, if you were to reduce their belief systems down to the fewest number of words, you would come up with Love. They all believed in Love.

Third, they were not the kind of people to put anyone down. You know in college, or in any community actually, there are these individuals many people view as bizarre or weird? The kind others will point at. Or laugh at behind their backs—even to their faces. These friends would never put another person down. They would extend the same level of respect to everyone as they would themselves want to receive.

Finally, with the exception of one, they were all sociology majors. They were attending Boston University to go out and become social workers. In other words, to dedicate their lives to improving the social conditions of those less fortunate. Even as an atheist, I recognized these friends believed in God without knowing it.

Harvey: When you talk about the Bible being infallible; the Bible can only be as infallible as the person interpreting it.

Marvin: Amen to that.

Rico: I hate to break up this lively discussion gentlemen, but Pete needs to do a sound check. What do you say we warm-up? After that we need to start getting into costume.

As the others gather themselves and head upstairs, I do a final check on the costumes and the props—a cardboard horse Rico will 'ride' onto stage and the lance he will carry, a lance covered with logos from McDonald's, Coca Cola, J.P. Morgan, and others. When I slip upstairs, I sit in the front row watching and listening to the troupe jam, pretty much as they did at camp. With Jamal playing bass and Rico on keyboards, their sound is fuller, more complex than when they were camping—especially with Andrew laying down polyrhythms on an Indian tabla. When someone comes to tape off the first few rows for reserved seating, I move toward the back of the auditorium, eventually wandering into the lobby.

Tom Cavanaugh and a few staff are setting up tables, stacking programs and other literature related to the Temple's other events. Two men stand near the entrance, dressed in suits and keeping to themselves. One stands with his arms crossed, the other occasionally peers out the glass doors. I re-enter the auditorium, visiting Pete in the sound booth. He smiles, occasionally making minor adjustments on the sound board.

When I decide to get some fresh air, I step outside where the two men I noticed earlier confront the drivers of two vehicles idling across the street. Judging from the body language, the conversations are animated, especially with the first driver. Eventually both vehicles pull away, one driver giving the two men the finger.

To my right, across the street under some trees, a small group is gathering, several wielding picket signs under their arms. I linger, watching early arrivals mount the steps and enter the Temple. Several I recognize from the park, a few smiling my way. Across the street, the group, though still small, increase in number. I decide to saunter nearer.

Most are middle-aged women though the more animate and vocal among them are younger, perhaps in their late 20's or early 30's. Among the men is, I assume, a priest or reverend. Many seem to defer to him as he struts among them, a bullhorn dangling in one hand.

The sidewalk fills with more people in groups of twos and threes, sometimes a full family unit, heading towards the Temple of (Wo)Man. I scan the picket signs:

Keep America Great – Keep Immigrants Out; *Beware of the BEAST, Satan Quotes Scripture*; *Willing to Fight (Die) to Defend Our Rights*, this one with an AR-15 decal prominently displayed. As the man with the bullhorn begins to corral his followers, attempting to organize them before they march en masse toward the Temple, I leave. I mount the steps, noting one of the two cars from earlier cruise by. I hurry through the lobby and the half-filled auditorium to join the others in the basement.

Some of the troupe are dressed, others still getting into costume. I meet the three guest speakers for the evening: a man introducing himself as Peter Hawkman; another, Sanjay Salim who is East Indian; the third, a tall, thin scarecrow of a woman named Aurora Hope. Hawkman is tall and thin, his long face beginning to wrinkle, his close-cropped hair sprouting a touch of gray. Salim is short by contrast, his dark bronze face a perfect circle, his head balding such that only a few tiny hairs remain on top. His accent is crisp, his speech clipped, his diction perfect.

Each is explaining the gist of their presentations to the troupe. Harvey, Jamal, and Rico listen attentively as Marvin flips through his poetry binder, occasionally extracting a page, then flipping through more pages. A few he hands to the others; most he keeps for himself.

More talkative than the others, Hope elaborates on her topic which is Human Transformation: the crucial need for the human race to make a paradigm shift in its thinking. Otherwise, she asserts, the impending challenges of global warming, human overpopulation, mass shootings, opioid addiction, political discord, etc. will completely overwhelm our self-indulgent, ill-equipped species.

All things, she says, in the outer world are reflections—are effects—of consciousness. Only when the mind itself is transformed do our lives achieve any significant change. Our thoughts, our words, and certainly our behavior, set off forces in the universe; everything being connected.

Harvey nods vigorously. It's a sad statement, he says, that it always takes a crisis for humans to abandon our petty differences and work together.

Wouldn't it be better, Hope suggests, if we not only join to combat the ill-effects of global warming, but also commit as a species—as a planet—on a common direction for all humanity to aspire towards? If each of us commits to making the world better than we found it; each in his or her own way. If we make government not about Big Brother but rather a vehicle to foster greater community and manifest our higher aspirations.

Harvey: You mean form a more perfect union?

Hope: Yes. Yes. Form a more perfect union.

Jamal references a Dr. Martin Luther King quote on the necessity for humanity to rise above its individualistic concerns to the broader concern of all humanity.

Marvin mentions Robert F. Kennedy, specifically his lament of American culture surrendering personal excellence and community values for the mere accumulation of material pursuits.

Every thought is based on either love or fear, Hope asserts. The task ahead is for the human race to become a human family, every neighborhood a close-knit community. Only a massive change of heart will change our societal direction in any significant way.

How realistic is that? Andrew asks, with more than eight billion inhabiting the planet, hundreds of millions of those struggling to merely survive?

Before Hope can respond, Tom Cavanaugh bounds down the stairs.

Ten minutes till curtain, he calls.

Now comes a time
to seek higher ground

IX

Now comes a time to seek higher ground
against that arrogant frown   swearing
an oath to a Constitution he systematically undermines
As loyalty   blind   whitewashes power's abuse
and whatever else   the Fox's News   can make stick
*   (Rule of law raped by a felony's prick*
while the Pontius Pilates in your Senate   genuflect)
Lucifer toasting marshmallows on the pyre
These are the times to try men's souls
The climate changing, forests on fire
Global warming   the moneychangers deny
To be silent is to consent
to the coming winter of growing discontent
as advocates of   Me   First
turn their backs on   We   the People
to build another biblical steeple
this one of crypto-currency and bit-coin
There is nothing new under the sun

After Tom Cavanaugh officially welcomes the audience, acknowledges the donors funding the event and urges everyone to silence their cell phones, the lights dim.

Shadows enter: the troupe moving across stage, getting into place. Their silhouettes in position, a swirling sound emanates from the surround-sound speakers. The swirl suggests wind fiercely circling the auditorium, at first rapidly, then slowing to a less frantic pace. A low drone, just barely audible, is added. It rises incrementally in volume. The two sounds linger for a long drawn-out moment. Then a new sound, like a rocket ship approaching, then lowering, followed by loud metallic clanking and a final startling clunk, loud enough that some in the audience startle.

The swirl of wind lessens as a slow, primitive yet pulsing drumbeat emerges, reinforced by the low, warm tones of Jamal's bass. Electric guitar is added. The swirling dissipates as a more upbeat, toe-tapping tempo takes over. A spotlight moves slowly downstage where it ascends a backdrop of clouds hovering over white-peaked mountains—the sun announcing the break of day.

The stage lights rise to reveal Jamal on a high chair, leaning over his bass, Harvey strumming his guitar and Andrew on a raised platform tapping a djembe while surrounded by a sea of hand percussion. To his right, raised even higher, as if on a mountain ledge, is Marvin, his back pressed against a simulated boulder. Marvin is dressed in a long off-white tunic, barefoot, his dark curly hair an illuminated halo, his facial expression one of remorse, his head frequently shaking. At times he deliberately turns his back to the audience.

The music shifts, going softer as a violin is heard. Entering from the right are Rico, a cardboard horse dangling from one shoulder, and Rikki wearing a monk's cassock. Rico's face is obscured by a knight's helmet. In one hand, he wields the lance. Rikki walks several feet behind, playing melancholy notes while Rico as Don Quixote shakes his head and shuffles despairingly toward center stage.

Off-mic Marvin shouts as if addressing the sky:

Oh, Don Quixote, what have you done?
You have slain the dragon
Burned its carcass in the sun
You have hacked its limbs
Its belly axed into 20 parts
But oh, Don Quixote
You have left intact its heart

Rico begins a litany of the year's mass shootings, providing dates, locations, and the number killed. Rikki's violin oozes sorrow, Rico's voice equally pained. When he pauses, Jamal leans into a microphone.

Our thoughts and prayers go out to the families of the victims, Jamal intones.

Harvey inserts: Insanity; definition: the doing of the same thing over and over yet hoping for a different result.

Rico continues his litany. He is joined by a recorded voice listing mass shootings from previous years, the two voices competing and overlapping. Marvin stands, facing the audience as Rico and the recorded voice lower in volume. Marvin shouts:

> *Though you've slit its wrists*
> *Gouged its eyes, shred its tongue*
> *Snapped its head off with a twist*
> *Though scale by green and wicked scale*
> *You have sliced the beast apart*
> *Oh, Don Quixote*
> *You have left intact its heart*

Jamal: Our thoughts and prayers go out to the families of the victims.

Harvey: Insanity, doing the same thing over and over yet hoping for a different result.

Rico's voice re-emerges as does the recorded voice. When he comes to the last mass shooting, one I recognize from the recent news, Rikki solos on violin. As her notes drift off, Marvin adds:

> *Knee-deep in red rivers*
> *He feeds his fledgling crop*
> *Oh, Don Quixote,*
> *This dragon is a clever fox.*

> *Its claws now nuclear iron*
> *Its teeth of stainless steel*
> *Its mating call: the screeching siren*
> *While tombstones shake their heads in disgust*
> *Oh, Don Quixote*
> *Can we ever slay the dragon that is us?*

Rikki brings up her violin. Rico discards his horse and lance, removes his helmet and steps behind his keyboards. The music fades. Just before we, the audience are prepared to applaud, Harvey starts a new tune.

The song is from the 60's, the lyrics from the Book of Ecclesiastes.

> *To everything. . .turn, turn, turn*
> *There is a season. . .turn, turn, turn*
> *And a time to every purpose under Heaven.*
> *A time to be born, a time to die. . .*

The others join in. Andrew switches to tabla, Marvin shakes a rain-stick, Jamal and Rico sing the chorus. As the song ends, Hawkman strolls onto stage.

He steps to a podium positioned center left, opposite where Rikki is playing violin. The music fades though not entirely. Light background music continues as Hawkman begins his own litany, this one of natural disasters caused by climate change. He names wildfires, severe storms and hurricanes, droughts, floods, the recent death toll around the globe due to record high temperatures. He likens the damage to the plagues visited on Egypt in the time of Moses. He likens the Pharaoh to current climate change deniers who refuse to heed or even acknowledge the warnings and mounting destruction.

Harvey: Insanity, doing of the same thing over and over yet hoping for a different result.

Our Mother is hurting, Hawkman continues. She is in pain, and screaming.

He likens the Earth to the human body. How the body when infected defends itself: producing antibodies, raising its temperature, vomiting, sneezing, coughing to expel the offending bacteria. Likewise, the Earth, he asserts, is trying to cast off its offending virus—a virus threatening her well-being and the existence of her many children.

A pacing Marvin interrupts from his mountain top:

> mother is angry, she is hurting. screaming in pain.
> she spits fire, shouts hurricanes,
> sends microscopic beetles to infest her better-dressed rats,
> her oceans of love now polluted with plastics
> her very breath a halitosis of hungry, homeless children
> her breast milk weighed by trauma
> shedding glass tears, her pride now windows into despair
> her toes tapping to the staccato of a spastic clock
> the algorithms of endangered species lining her fears.

Earth is hurting, Hawkman continues. He cites endangered species going extinct at an unprecedented rate; the vanishing coral reefs; the thinning of the Earth's ozone layer with the rise in carbon emissions. He cites the garbage patch in the Pacific Ocean twice the size of Texas; similar patches in the South Pacific, the North and South Atlantic and Indian Oceans. He cites the mounting toll of human death and disaster as a consequence of global warming, a toll that can only rise until we humans change our behavior.

Marvin:

> the sin of overabundance is exacting its bill
> the cacophony of contradictions sounding its timpani
> the march of history repeating itself like an anorexic,
> two fingers down the throat, on bare knees,
> poised over the spit-polished toilet

> I push my granddaughter on a swing,
> teach her to tie her shoes,
> show her the miracle of growing things
> the world she's inheriting is withering on its vine,
> her once great grandmother wincing in agony,
> across the street, cranes and compressors

> Ares wears a hardhat, running a cement mixer
> his buddies laying bricks, a subcontractor
> cutting into logs the last of the trees

Harvey sings in the background:

To everything. . .turn, turn, turn,
There is a season. . .turn, turn, turn

Though the situation is dire, Hawkman says, there is hope.

There is always hope, he repeats.

He speaks of the international group he heads—scholars, graduate students and environmentalists who have identified more than a hundred ways humans can individually and collectively effectively reduce carbon emissions. He cites a handout available in the lobby. He likens the fossil fuel industry to the tobacco industry decades ago, as well as the current gun lobby. Despite the increasingly obvious truth that smoking caused lung cancer, despite the burning of fossil fuels and the cutting down of forests wreaking havoc on our air, despite the easy availability of guns and especially assault weapons resulting in gun violence being the leading cause of death in America, these organizations deny, obfuscate and bury data, more concerned with protecting their profit margin over preserving and enhancing the quality of human life.

Harvey shouts:

Who was it who said, *love of money*
is the root of all evil?

Marvin inserts:
Ares rubs the stubble on his cheeks
his plaid shirt rolled up at the sleeves
the tattoos on his biceps a dull green
his buddies march in black boots, pump fists,
there is nothing new under the pulsing sun

you stand on the last pages of a closing chapter
the afternoon sun burns holes in your fragile optimism
mother complains of an ache in her chest.

her heart beat slowing, smoke fills her eyes,
mudslides clog her arteries.
boxed in a concrete canyon, she lashes out,
writhing in pain as she inflicts the same
with thunderous rapidity
Ares, wearing earplugs, doesn't hear a thing.

But most importantly, Hawkman continues, the human species is in need of a major paradigm shift. No longer can our thinking, our attitude, be human-centric—measured in terms of human comfort, convenience, and capital gain. Like the indigenous people of this country who we nearly turned into an endangered species, we must recognize we, all life on this planet, are a family, living in a symbiotic relationship; each member of that family dependent on all other members of that same family. Should we fail not to shift our perspective, the Earth will continue to cast off as many of us as she can. . .until we are either annihilated or humbly submit to the devastating lesson she is desperately trying to teach us.

Marvin:

a beer after hours. weekends at the shooting range,
Ares spits on his finger to test the wind
prays for a self-fulfilling prophecy,
a challenge to all he has become
may the gods and not its furies be with him

"higher, grandpa!" my granddaughter commands.
I give another shove. remember your asthma,
I think to say. . .instead, I say nothing.

Marvin turns his back.

Harvey:

To everything. . .turn, turn, turn. . .

As Harvey ends the chorus, the others singing along, Hawkman exits the stage to thunderous applause.

Salim enters as Hawkman leaves. He stands behind the podium. He watches the audience as the music and the applause fade to silence. He allows the silence to linger. He lowers his head, folds his hands as if in prayer. Coughing and seat-shifting emanate from the audience till the silence becomes uncomfortable. Finally, he begins.

As I stand here, there are more than 8 billion people on this planet, he says. Eight billion people. I ask this question: How many billion will be enough? How many will be too much? Ten billion? 20 billion? Thirty? The previous speaker spoke about climate change: how for decades, we have collectively denied human activity has been adversely affecting the health of our planet. Now we find ourselves in a situation where we can no longer afford to deny what we know in our hearts to be true—*have known* in our hearts to be true.

It may be too late. Even if we do come to a point where we are able to stop and possibly reverse the adverse effects of climate change, it won't come without the loss of millions, perhaps a billion lives—and trillions of dollars, which for some, matters far more than all those lives lost.

Just as we have been denying the existence of global warming, we have been denying there are *already* way too many people populating this planet. Let me repeat that: *there are already too many people populating our planet.* As I speak, there are 35 million refugees around the globe. Thirty-five million. People who for one reason or another have been forced or chose to leave their homeland to find a more hospitable place to live. Struggling in one way or another to eke out a living, hoping to eventually find a home. Thirty-five million. The United States is not the only country with hordes of desperate immigrants trying to cross its borders.

Now add to these the homeless. In this country alone, more than half a million. That number steadily increasing. Half a million and counting with no place to live.

Might these statistics suggest there are already too many people on the planet?

Let me ask you this? Where in this great country of yours are the most crimes being committed? Where is the highest concentration of mental illness and aberrant behavior? Isn't it in your more crowded cities? This nation recently reached the milestone where more people now live in cities than in small towns and rural areas. Do you think this will lead to less crime or more? To less mental illness or more? Given the social and mental problems greater density of human beings cause, does it make more sense to add to the human population? Or to reduce it?

I ask another question. What do you think will happen to human society when the world population reaches 15 or 20 billion? Will we adapt to accommodate that expanding number? Will each of us volunteer to consume less, both because the earth's resources will by then be considerably less, and also because consuming less will be the only way an expanding population can exist?

Or will we do what we have done for centuries? Kill each other over territory and the earth's limited resources. Survival of the fittest, the law of the bully, the mafia of greed.

One alternative might be to devalue human life. Although we currently give lip service to the idea that all human life is precious—that all are endowed with certain inalienable rights—perhaps we will come to re-evaluate that notion. We might decide to no longer strive to extend human life as we currently do. Since our older citizens are going to die relatively soon anyway, and are an increasing drain on our medical system, perhaps we should decline to extend their lives any longer than is economically advantageous. Wouldn't all that money being spent on people who have ceased being productive members of society, be better spent elsewhere?

Then too, maybe we'll resort to making assisted suicide a profit-making venture. Create a new industry for those seeking another means to earn a buck. Think of the job opportunities!

Abortion—which some in this country are trying to ban outright—might again be made perfectly legal, even encouraged; perhaps state sponsored and financed. Some cultures might limit the number of births, or support sterilizing women after the second or third child. Others might return to the ancient practice of killing females at birth as the fewer females a population has, the fewer children they can produce.

I, of course, am giving you a very bleak scenario. Perhaps we will get lucky. Maybe Mother Nature will curb the human population for us. As forest fires, hurricanes, floods, droughts, and record temperatures increase, maybe the death toll from natural disasters will rise enough to balance or at least slow population growth enough that we as a species will come to tolerate these ever-increasing disasters. No? You don't like that idea? Don't think that might happen?

Here's one more alternative. Rather than deny there might already be too many people on the planet; rather than not acknowledge that should we continue the way things are currently going, things can only get worse before there is any hope of them getting better—we instead pledge to work conscientiously and deliberately to reduce the human population in responsible, humane, non-obtrusive ways. Begin with aiming for zero population growth. Achieving that, then aim to reduce the total population. Make reduction of the number of refugees worldwide the litmus test. Aim to reduce the homeless camping out on our streets. Aim for a world where as many as possible can meet their basic needs rather than a world that keeps adding more and more bodies to the growing pile of endless human suffering.

As Salim speaks, Rico's synthesizer churns an off-rhythm, ambient muddle of sounds to which Andrew and Marvin add random percussion. Gradually, bass and guitar are introduced while the synthesized cacophony fades. As Salim finishes, stepping away from the mic, Andrew run his fingers along a set of chimes.

Immediately the lights go out, a single spotlight focused on Marvin, his figure bent and contorted.

Marvin:

We hold these truths to be self-evident
That all men are created equal

The music shifts, each musician transitioning, falling in sync.

We hold these truths to be self-evident
That all men and all women are created equal

We hold these truths to be self-evident
That all men and all women
And all chimpanzees and all orangutans
And all elephants and all lions and all tigers
And all hyenas and all antelope and all zebra
And all sharks and whales and all dolphins
And all larks and eagles and all pigeons and all worms
*   and all lizards*
And all mosquitoes and all tsetse flies
Are endowed by their Creator with certain inalienable rights
That among these be life, liberty, and the pursuit of
*   happiness*

The music rises, Andrew pounding his djembe, Jamal locked in on bass; guitar and synthesizer adding melodic touches, Rikki playing pizzicato on her violin.

Marvin:

To be or not to be,
That is the question
Whether 'tis nobler in the mind to suffer
The slings and arrows of outrageous fortune
Or to take arms against a sea of troubles
And by opposing. . .

Jamal:

To form a more perfect union
Establish Justice, insure domestic tranquility
Provide for the common defense
Promote the general welfare
And secure the blessings of Liberty
To ourselves and our Posterity. . .

Marvin:

. . .or not

Marvin shrugs, turns his back only to wheel around again.

To be or not to be
Whether to make it all about ME
Or about WE. . .
Close the door on either/or
Make harmony of opposites. . .
To treat the Other as brother
In the knowledge that what you put out, comes back
One way . . .or another.

Jamal:

Ask not what your country can do for you. . .

Marvin:

Ask what you can do for your countrymen.

Jamal:

To be or not to be.

Marvin:

To be. . .or not to be

Both:

You choose.

As their music crescendos, the lights come up, everyone on stage illuminated. Marvin squats, shaking his head, burying his head in his hands, turning his back.
Jamal:

I come from a dysfunctional family.
my mother, a committed democrat, strives for consensus,
listening to all sides, hoping to smooth over
entrenched family antagonisms

my father, lifelong libertarian, knows right is right,
he the lucky keeper of wisdom's keys,
his knees bloodied on complacent arrogance

my sisters all cling to some version of themselves,
stalking the malls, marinating rumors while getting
*   their hair done,*
criticizing the competition, backstabbing whichever sister
has the richest husband   or handsomest lover

my brothers like to fist-fight and wrestle to determine
which can withstand the most pain
and therefore be most worthy to dish pain out

I've aunts who chain-smoke conspiracy theories,
donate to Jesus and religious cults that promise
Heaven's cleanest dishes

my uncles all suffer PTSD, confusing the enemies

they once obliterated with our houseboy,
the kitchen help, our Latino gardener,
          those teenage immigrants bouncing basketballs
as they allegedly stake out our upstairs

my cousins carry picket signs my other cousins,
those living in the country, use for target practice

Rico:

our house is in shambles,
the foundation consumed by termites,
the wallpaper stained and peeling,
hurricanes rattle our shutters,
forest fires send smoke signals that rub against our windows,
slither through cracks, under and around warped door frames

on creaking steps, dad slaps mom silly
my siblings argue over who gets what leftovers
past due notices pile up but dad refuses to pay the mortgage
ever since mom called the police on him

the officers are dad's poker buddies,
best men at their wedding, still
mom refuses to drop the charges
we siblings hedge our bets over whose side to take

Aurora Hope enters. She strides to the podium and adjusts the mic as the music slowly fades, replaced by the faint sound of a steady heartbeat. A minute into Hope's talk, Rikki bows her violin.

Acknowledging the bleak picture both Hawkman and Salim painted, Hope sighs. How easy, she warns, how tempting to want to throw up one's hands, to feel help-less, to give up. To decide there is little-to-nothing any of us can do to avoid the self-made precipice we seem poised to tumble over. But there is a solution, she says. A simple solution.

All you need is love.

We can decide right now, as a people, as a

nation, as a species, whether we continue to serve the god of money—which is what we have been doing, allowing our economy to dictate the direction society goes in—or serve the God of Love.

What if our corporations voluntarily placed human values above economic ones? she suggests. Placed our *common* wealth over their own? What if their business model, rather than solely increasing the well-being of their stockholders and their CEOs, was centered around making our communal existence better? Spreading the wealth we collectively generate such that everyone of us sits at the table of that common prosperity? What if gun manufacturers valued human life and the safety of children far above the fattening of their own wallets?

All you need is Love.

Just that shift in our collective thinking, our collective values, would do worlds to end the current dilemma we find ourselves in. Merely choosing Love over pride, ego, fear, and greed. What if each religion centered again on that essential message?

Andrew toots on a wooden flute. Rikki responds by plucking her violin. As their notes playfully dance around each other, the steady heartbeat in the background rises in volume.

Hope: What if our country, our civilization made love of its children, *their* health, *their* education, *their* well-being its absolute highest priority? What if our economy was geared to, above all else, nurture *them*? After all, are they not only our future, but the greatest hope our species has to avoid what scientists warn could be this planet's 6th extinction? They are the ones who must finish the job we thus far seem incapable of even beginning to address. What if we made *their* preparedness and emotional stability this nation's number one focus? I can guarantee you: all our material needs could not help but be met in the process. I can guarantee you, all of God's goodness and mercy couldn't help but to rain down on us like manna.

Marvin:

Somewhere between mud and heaven.
This forgetting, this never knowing the known
This denying what like bone permeates our imperviousness
to WE

Harvey:

Who was it who said, Love of money is the root of all evil?

Jamal:

Who are they who say the second amendment
should trump the sixth commandment?

Marvin:

Somewhere between dirt and stratosphere
The right to take away what cannot be taken
Except on pain of inflicting pain
which always returns to haunt
To hang somewhere between rock and ruin.

Hope: To change our current trajectory, we need merely to recognize what we do to anyone, we do to ourselves. What we put out in the world comes back to us. In one way or another. It always comes back. That is the law of the universe. It is the law of Karma. It is the law of God.

Ask yourselves: When you put out Love, what is it you get back in return? Isn't it Love? And when you put out fear, or anger, or hatred, what is it you get back in return? If you treat others as lesser than yourself, what can you expect to get back from them? And when you treat an other like family, what do they give *you* in return?

I say it again: All you need is Love.

Marvin: All you need is Love

The others: All you need is Love.

Hope pauses as the music transitions. Harvey sings the old Beatles song of the same name. After a few verses, the music is brought down, Harvey continuing to hum the melody.

I feel I must address the importance of supporting and educating young girls and women, Hope then says, asking those of the Muslim faith in particular to heed her words. She recounts her experience in third-world countries, heading organizations providing small grants to those struggling to improve their lives. Whereas men, she says, gravitate toward grandiose plans to lift themselves out of poverty, dreaming of that magical land called success, women used the funds for things closer to home, improving the conditions for their families and their immediate environment, their success rate significantly higher than their male counterparts.

She further asserts the male consciousness as being prone to seek dominance. The patriarchal approach is one that seeks to impose its will on others. Women lean more towards healing and nurturing and are thus prone to seek harmony. Healing the Earth, she says, must take precedence over the masculine tendency to force the Earth to serve us. What if society's primary purpose, after its children, is to nurture the Earth? To give back to our common Mother that her beauteous bounty be restored and her many fruits once again flourish uncontaminated? Surely the end result can only improve our collective lives as well.

Marvin:

We stand on the western edge of all there is.
Like a stubborn zipper, PTSD of the moral compass,
*   the American Dream is on anti-depressants.*
The first half of the 20th century again rears
*   its broken rhyme.*

The logarithms of circular self-interest
*   whip its urgent branches as we the people*
*   lose parts of ourselves.*

A familiar dark illuminates the black hole
of our collective lack of conscience.
Evangelicals hold Jesus in a headlock.
The lamppost of wisdom flickers through a prismed glass.
In its wake, mass shootings,   a red dawn
paranoia attempting to manage two horizons at once.
Life weaves its contradictions into a French twist.
Common sense follows the stale bread crumbs.

Hope again speaks of Karma, how the world we create is a reflection of what we put out, our thoughts and our actions. She warns of our cultural tendency to glorify violence in our movies and video games—that violence now manifesting in our political discourse as well as our streets. She recommends we move away from violence as entertainment as it can only reinforce the darker aspects of our nature. Movies, entertainment that resolve conflict through love, patience, understanding and above all, *listening,* would better aid future generations in resolving and correcting the errors our and previous generations have foisted upon them.

Harvey sings All you need is love, completing the final verse.

Marvin:

Step out of the cave of deep sleep,
the river of cliché,
the logic of barbed wire stitching conspiracies
out of the ding and dangle of disappointment,
*   out of thin fear.*

Harvey:

Do unto others what you would have them do unto you

Marvin:

This is what the Christians say. But Confucius said that too
Do not do unto others what you would not have them do
unto you

Harvey:

Tho they say it different ways; it's the same Golden Rule

Marvin:

Hurt not others in ways you yourself would find hurtful

Harvey:

This is how the Buddhists have it phrased

Marvin:

While the Hindus say: If you do naught to others
what you would not have them do to you, you'll be happy
all your days

Both:

Could this really be true?
Do both us and they believe the same Golden Rule?

Harvey:

Desire for your brother what you would have him desire
for you

Marvin:

This is what the Muslims say. But the Indians believe that too

Harvey:

Let me not judge my neighbor
till I've walked a mile in his shoes
Tho we say it different ways; it's the same Golden Rule

Marvin:

What is hateful to you do not do unto your neighbor

Harvey:

That's the law and the wisdom of the Jews

Marvin:

*Regard your neighbor's gain as your own,
his loss as your loss too*
Harvey:

*The Taoists say that.
Tho we say it different ways;
it's the same Golden Rule*

Marvin:

All you need is. . .

Two loud pops come from the other side of the auditorium. I see Marvin jolt and fall backwards. At first, I think it's part of their act, till pandemonium sweeps through the crowd. I see Marvin roll then crawl behind the cardboard boulder. A tussle breaks out. People are apparently trying to subdue a lone gunman. Those on stage either drop or watch in horror. Marvin waves a hand and calls he's okay. Just as the assailant is forced to the ground, a loud crash emanates from the rear of the auditorium. Loud machine gun fire erupts. I turn, intending to duck, but not quick enough. I feel a sharp sting. As I fall, blood gurgling from my neck, those around me crouch in terror, the woman nearest me covering her mouth, weeping, and shaking her head...

X

ACKNOWLEDGEMENTS

My greatest thanks to my darling wife, Colette, whose love and unwavering support has allowed me to indulge the creative impulses that have resulted in this as well as earlier works. A sincere thanks to Joseph Cavanaugh whose insights have made this work substantially richer than the original manuscript I submitted. Thanks also to friend, Faye Quam, for her proofreading and editing skills. And further thanks to Mark Terry whose steady hand and keen mind has kept this boat afloat until it is here, finally brought to shore.

Final thanks to those many, many friends and creative conspirators who have in countless ways made my creative journey far, far richer than it would have been had I made the journey alone.

Bless you every one.

ABOUT THE AUTHOR

Gregory Seth Harris, aka *Seth,* is one of Colorado's best known performance poets. A poet and experimental writer, SETH is author of the absurdist satire, *The Perfect Stranger,* a Kafkaesque examination of human folly and the folly of human institutions. His poetic memoir, *A Black Odyssey,* is modeled after Homer's classic epic, using it as an allegorical scaffolding for his own experience as a Black Man in contemporary America. His experimental short fiction has appeared in numerous literary journals including *Fugue*, *Portland Review*, *Lynx Eye* and *Happy*.

Also a musician and actor, SETH has collaborated with countless musicians, poets, actors, dancers and other performance artists. Living in Denver, CO, he is the founder of the musical-poetic ensemble, *Art Compost & the Word Mechanics*. An audiobook of *A Black Odyssey*, the entire collection performed with *Art Compost* is available where most audiobooks are sold. Visit **SETH & Art Compost** on Facebook or YouTube for video performances.

Learn more at www.wagingart.com.

The author's best friend.

Mark Terry

Joe Cavanaugh

We are poets and writers publishing poets and writers, focused on both the smallest detail and the far horizon.

If you are looking for a publisher to share your passion for writing, one that understands that every word matters and quality drives success, we are here for you.

Contact:

Joe Cavanaugh
jcavanaugh1@gmail.com

Mark Terry
markajterry@gmail.com